DRIVING WILD

THE DRIVING SERIES
BOOK TWO

HALEY COOK

SOUTHERN LIBRARIAN PUBLISHING

Formatting by HC PA & Formatting Services

Cover Design by Sammie Bee Designs

Cadwallader Photography

Model: Storm Wilson

Editing by Kat Wyeth (Kat's Literary Services)

Proofreading by Louise Murphy (Kats Literary Services)

ISBN: 9798883907929

ISBN: 9798324069469

❀ Created with Vellum

DRIVING *Wild*

HALEY COOK

CONTENTS

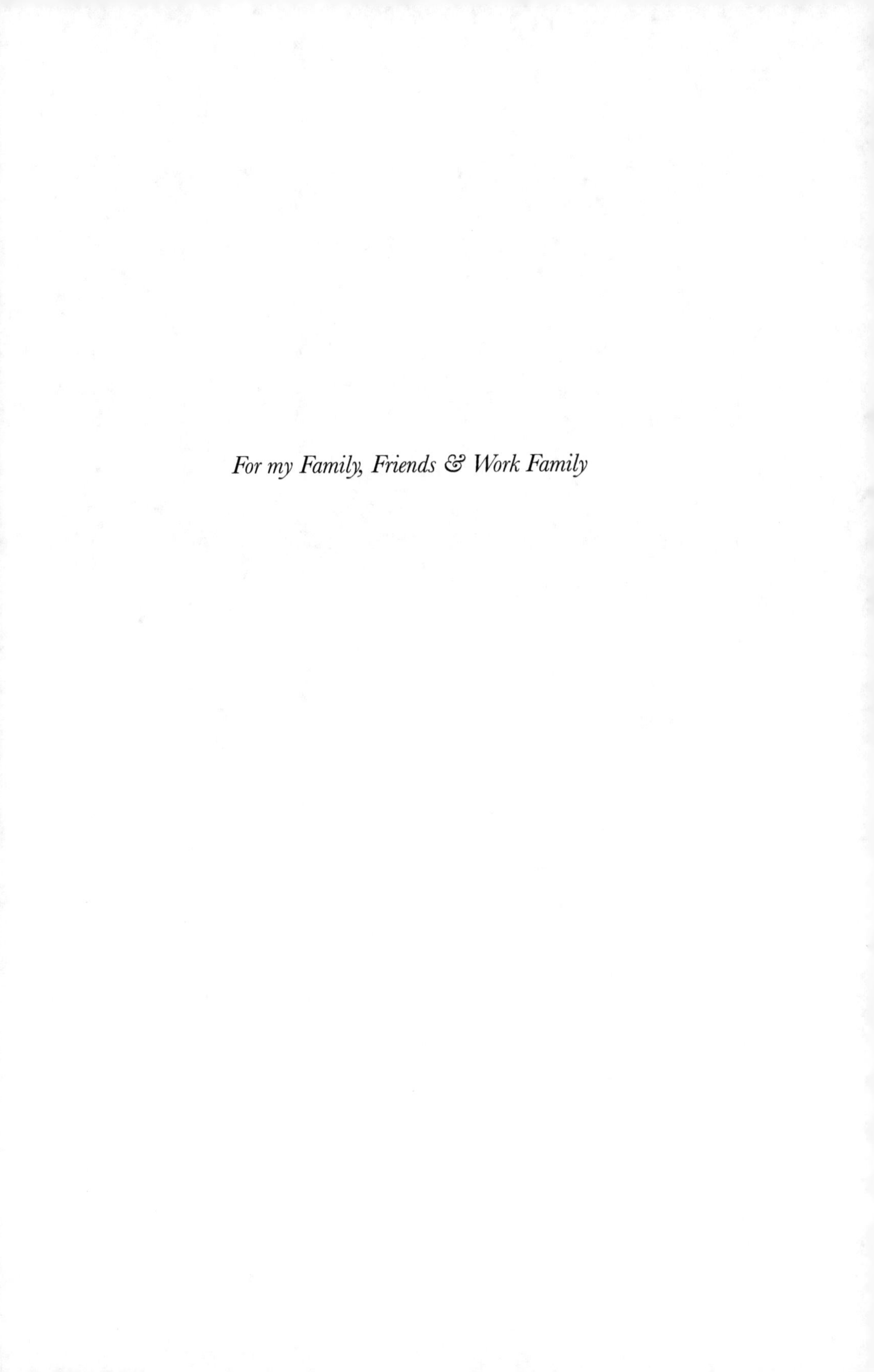

For my Family, Friends & Work Family

Chapter 1
Matt

"Well, what do we have here?" my best friend says. Groaning, I roll over just as he comes into view. The room is dark from the curtains being pulled closed, so it takes a little for my eyes to adjust to him turning on the bedside lamp.

"What the hell do you want? It's too early for you to be this happy."

"Oh, I'm just here to make sure that you get up and get to the shop on time."

"What are you talking about? I'm always on time." Sitting up a little too quickly, my head pounds from the night before. What was in those drinks that woman kept giving me? And my next question is why in the hell had I kept accepting them?

Ryan stopped dead in his tracks like he's seen a ghost. "Matt, man, have you looked at the person next to you?" I slowly turn my head, trying not to make too much of an abrupt movement that's going to send me running to the bathroom from the way my head pounds. Shit! Resting my head on my knees, this is not at all the way I thought my night would have gone. Then I notice the smug look on his face. "You better get your ass out of that bed now because Tinley is going to lose her shit when she finds Grace here." Shrugging, I pull the covers off as I try to figure out what happened last night and how I ended up with Grace in my bed.

"Well, thank God you have underwear on, bud. I really don't need to see all of you this early in the morning," Ryan says.

Slowly shaking my head to try to get my bearings, I don't even remember talking to Grace, let alone bringing her back to my apartment. When I pulled the covers back, I noticed she still had all her clothes on from the night before. There is no way we did anything. I mean, I would remember doing something with her. She is just that hot. The woman has been living rent-free in my head for months. We had one ridiculously hot, hate-filled night at the track when I happened to stumble into her coming out of Ryan's trailer after seeing Tinley one weekend. She'd broken up with her long-term boyfriend a few weeks before. Even with the fact of knowing she was using me to get over him, honestly, I didn't care. I'd had a shitty race weekend and needed a release. It was one of the hottest nights I'd had in a long time. And since then, I could go for a repeat, but she's made it clear that she sees me as a playboy or, as she called me, a fuckboy on all levels. I drag my eyes slowly away from her perfect ass that's barely covered in the skirt she's wearing.

"Come on, bud, go shower because you smell like a brewery. We can figure this out on our way to work. I'll get the coffee going because I have a feeling you're going to need it after what I just walked in on."

A few minutes later, I'm standing in the shower, water pelting me as I try to remember what happened last night, and nothing is coming. Why can't I remember anything after getting a beer at the bar? Just as I start to wash my hair, I glance down at my hand.

WHAT THE FUCK?

I stare at my left hand, trying to figure out exactly why I have a platinum band on my ring finger and who I could be married to. Standing under the shower for longer than humanly necessary, the water has turned cold, and I take that as my incentive to get out. Only to be confronted by the one woman who I can't for the life of me figure out if I'm married to or not.

I stumble to grab a towel and get my bearings. Grace stands in front of me with a look that most men would bow down to, but little does she know, I'm not that man, and it'll take a lot more than a gorgeous set of legs and a smart mouth to make me bow, even though The General is trying to tell me differently. But we have some other issues that need to be addressed.

"What the hell, Matt McCall?" Grace practically yells at me, making me rub my temples; my head's about to explode.

Giving her a once-over, the woman is gorgeous, with platinum blonde hair that she's decided to cut off and long legs that I want wrapped around me again. She's missing her red lipstick. Those perfect lips have driven me wild since day one. So hot and vibrant, making her nickname so easy. But she's such a natural beauty that she doesn't even need it.

"I was hoping you could tell me, Red, because just as I was taking a shower, I noticed I'm wearing a piece of jewelry that sure as hell wasn't on my finger yesterday before I went out." Crossing my arms over my bare chest and putting the noticeable ring on display, I watch for any type of reaction from her. Nothing, and I do mean nothing, changes. This woman is going to be a pain in my ass, just as I thought.

"Well, I can tell you one damn thing—my left hand is bare, so you sure as hell didn't marry me. But for some ungodly reason, I woke up in your house with one of the worst headaches I think I've ever had. So I'm going to need *you* to fill in some blanks for me," she states.

I rub my head yet again in frustration at the way this morning is going.

"Red, if I could tell you why you're here, believe me, I would, but until Ryan came to get me so we could head to the shop, I didn't even know that I was in the world. The last I remember, I was talking to a dark-haired woman at a bar, and then *bam*, I woke up with a ring on my finger and you in my bed, so your guess is as good as mine. Now, if you will let me get ready, I've got to head to work. Not all of us can live on Daddy's money while we figure out what job suits us best.

Grace just stands in the doorway for a few more minutes until she makes a noise I'm sure only dogs can hear, and then she storms away.

By the time I finally get dressed and make it out to the kitchen, Ryan is waiting with a shit-eating grin on his face. Smacking him on the back of the head as I pass by, I reach for my coffee, which is now cold, of course, because I took longer than I should have, all because of the blonde-headed siren who stormed into my bathroom.

"Care to explain now? What the hell happened, bud?" Ryan asks. Releasing a long breath, I pour the cold coffee into the sink and elect to make a new cup. Hitting the button on my coffee machine, I spin around to hold up my left hand. "Any chance in hell you might know why I have a ring on my left hand?" Ryan nearly chokes on his drink as he just stares at me.

"Wait, did you marry Grace? Is that why she was in your bed? Dude, North Carolina isn't like Vegas; you can't just go to any little white chapel on the corner and get married. I have so many questions and none of them start with *congratulations.*" Ryan continues with his little twenty questions as I try to finish drinking my coffee. But I hate to break the news to him: I don't have answers to any of them.

"Would you stop with the questions? I have zero, and I do mean zero, memory of last night, so I can't answer a damn thing." Grabbing the bottle of aspirin, I pop two in my mouth. "Let's go to work. We need to get ready for the race week."

Rolling my shoulders that are already so tense, I can tell it's going to result in me being in a crappy mood all day as we head down to my car. My baby is an orange Dodge Charger, just like Bo and Luke Duke had. I grew up in Alabama, so I'm a country boy all the way. This car is the one thing that I had to have when I made it into the Cup Series. Ryan hates it more than life itself, so that makes me love it even more. He thinks it's too loud and too noticeable to drive around town, but I love it. "Get in the car, asswipe. I'm driving. You can leave your truck here," I tell him. Having the Twilight Zone morning I've had, it's the least he can do for me.

"Okay, one last question, then we can go. I just need to know one thing. Have you and Grace hooked up before, or is this just an 'I was drunk and she helped me get home' type of thing?" he asks.

With a smirk, I slide into my seat and bring my baby to life with a roar.

"You didn't answer my question, asswipe."

"Sorry, can't hear you over the car." I turn onto the highway and head toward Mac Motorsports.

Walking into the shop, I'm met with some odd looks and hushed whispers. We make our way to where the crew chiefs' offices are located.

"Ryan, Matt, I need you both in my office," Brad says.

"Great, I haven't even done anything in months, and now I'm being called into the office with you. Thanks, man," Ryan states.

"Hey, I haven't done anything either. Well, not that I know of."

"Yeah, tell that to the ring on your left hand. And why are you still wearing it?" Ryan points out.

Shit. Shaking my head, I follow him into Brad's office. When the PR guys call you in, you always feel like you're in the principal's office because they usually only want to "talk" when you've done something to embarrass the company.

Walking into the office, Brad is at his desk, papers flooding it with stats, updates, image photos, and articles about the company. He's reading the morning paper as we take a seat across from him, so it can't be that bad if he's relaxed enough to read the paper, right?

"Brad, you wanted to see us."

"Yeah, I sure did. Just had a question for you both."

Bracing for what's to come, I look over at Ryan, who's as cool as a cucumber. With the way the media's been to him over the last few months, I'm sure he's not even worried about what they could say anymore. He and his now girlfriend, Tinley, have been put to the test over the last few months by an ex-girlfriend who had claimed that she was pregnant, only to have made the entire thing up to get extra attention for her career.

"First, let me get one thing back from you, Matt." Reaching his hand out, he says, "I'd like my ring. The wife didn't much care for me coming home without it last night. But I figured you needed it a little more than me from the way that woman wouldn't leave you alone."

Staring at Brad for a few minutes, I try to wrap my head around the fact that he was the one who put this ring on my hand. Working the ring off my finger, I hand it back to him and sit back in my chair, breathing a little easier now that I know I'm not married to some stranger.

"Well, with that little bit cleared up, any chance you might be able to tell me anything else about last night? The last thing that I could make out was the brunette giving me a drink, and then nothing."

"Well, that brunette was a reporter, and she was digging for information on the team. Things are starting to change around here, and I'm going to tell you both now. Starting next season, we are going to bring on a third driver, and it's going to be a female; her name is Mila. So somehow, that has gotten out, and you would think we're the royal family with how many phone calls I have received this week alone asking about it. The reporter must have thought she had a chance to get some answers out of you by getting you drunk. Luckily, Grace and Tinley happened to be coming for drinks at the same place and saw her putting something into a beer she bought you. So Grace stepped in and stated that she was your wife," Brad tells us.

But I'm so lost in my thoughts that Grace did something to help me that I can't begin to figure it out.

"So that's why I called you both in here. The reporter has now taken the story of you and the little missus and run with it. It's time for us to do some damage control."

I sit up and lean over so my head is in my hands, trying to wrap my brain around the events of last night.

"Let me get this straight, just so I can make sure I heard you correctly, okay?

"First, I was talking to a pretty woman who happened to be a reporter.

"Second, she put something in my beer to get me to talk about something that I had no idea was even happening until just now.

"Third, you gave your ring to Grace, which she then put on my finger and acted as if we were married.

"Yet Tinley said nothing to you about this whole scene when she got home?" I look over to Ryan who's just shaking his head like he has no idea what's going on either.

"Fourth, the press now think I am married and have decided that it is the most interesting thing today because the real reality stars have done nothing overnight for them to report, so they've resorted to talking about NASCAR drivers?

"Did I get all that correct?"

"That about breaks it all down," he confirms. "Now, I'm going to need some damage control from you. I don't want to babysit you because I have enough on my plate with the new driver coming in," Brad continues.

A knock pulls me from my thoughts.

Lifting my head, the woman in question walks in the door. I was raised to always be respectful and offer my seat to any female, but Grace has landed herself on my shit list. But of course, Ryan, being the good guy, offers her his.

"Okay, kids, I am going to say this once and then we are going to go about our day. Grace, I'm sure the team has caught you up to speed since you are going to be working here with our new driver coming in. Normally, the policy is that drivers are off-limits to date, but it looks like the little stunt you pulled to get the reporter away has now resulted in the press thinking you are married. So guess what we're going to do now?" Brad asks.

What the fuck? I am going to make Grace's life a living hell. She knew exactly why I had a ring on my hand. She was playing along with what happened, yet she said nothing. She let me spin out this morning, trying to figure out what happened.

"Back to my original purpose of calling you both in here. Mila will be coming in from New York in the next few weeks to get settled into joining the team. Also, she will be doing a few promotional things with the PR team. So I need you on your best behavior. I don't need extra attention on us when we already have this announcement coming. And I don't have the time nor the energy to get you out of the messes you seem to magically find yourself in," Brad says.

"Brad, do you really think this is necessary? You don't think the media will let it go, especially with the announcement coming about Mila?" Grace states.

"Honestly, I would love to say yes, that they will just move on, but I don't want to take the chance with all that's on the line coming up. I have spoken to the higher-ups, and they suggest we have you look like a model married couple for the next two months. That will give us time to put Mila in the spotlight and show that we are one big racing family. Since you're already a growing star within the sport, we also need to change the public opinion of you being a playboy. Time to grow up, son, and be a family man. Mila will need the help between you and Ryan coming into the male-dominated world. And Grace, with you working with her, this will be the perfect time for you to show that aspect," Brad explains.

"She's already coming from a family team to join ours, so what better way to show how connected everyone is?" he continues.

Turning to face my "wife," I can't help but feel on edge. She's been a pain in my ass for months with her remarks about the life I lead and being the fuckboy of NASCAR. But Grace is about to get the awakening of a lifetime with me as her husband.

"Well, this has been a great morning, but if you will excuse me, I need to get to work, and honestly, being called someone's husband wasn't high on the list of things to check off today," I say, standing up and heading toward the door. Turning around, I look at my beautiful, blonde bombshell of a fake wife and leave her with my parting words.

"See you later tonight, WIFE."

Chapter 2
Grace

Tinley had made the connection faster than I could about the woman being from a news outlet. I just reacted on instinct, jumping in to help, not even caring that Matt may be the bane of my existence.

Seeing Brad sitting with the other crew guys, I knew just what I needed to do. Did I want to tell Matt about it this morning when I woke up in his bed? The only reason I had been sleeping beside him this morning was because I was worried about the drug that reporter had put in the beer. I may have not wanted to play the part but I wasn't going let him choke and die either. Nope, that's why I played dumb and acted like I didn't know how I got there. I hadn't gotten to his beer quick enough before he took a few sips of it, so he was going to need help getting home. And after making the scene of him being my husband, I couldn't leave it to the crew guys to get him there.

I couldn't help but think that my first morning at Mac Motorsports was turning into a shit show. I thought I was just trying to be a nice person, a team player, by getting that ridiculous reporter away from Matt last night. Why did I have to put that ring on his finger? Now I'm tied to the one person I can't stand for the next two months. It rattles me so much, even being around him for longer than a cup of coffee seems like a lot. But also, he seems to be the only one who turns my insides on fire, making me break into a sweat when his amazing smell is near—spice and motor oil.

When I walked into my small office earlier, I hadn't even gotten the chance to get settled in before Brad called, letting me know what was going on. Little did he realize I've had Google Alerts on myself for as long as I can remember. Some people may think I'm conceited for that, but I couldn't care less. Those are the people who really don't know me. Coming from a family that has their name in a few different businesses across the country, it's just easier to stay ahead of the game. I'd already been on the phone with my father most of the morning. And that was about as fun as a vaginal exam this early in the morning. God forbid I put the wonderful Miller name into the gutter.

Miller Motorsports is the legacy my cousin, Jamie, is CEO of. It's a part of our family's many businesses. I was expected to join the company after finishing school at App State here in North Carolina. I fell in love with the state and have no interest in moving back home. It also helps that people don't care what my family name is or that we own a race team. Honestly, people never even make the connection since Miller is a very common name, and I make a point not to put myself in the press. I like being behind the scenes and getting to just be a normal twenty-two-year-old. I set my phone down, and it vibrates yet again on my desk. It has gone a little crazy in the group chat with my cousins since the news broke. Being an only child, I grew up close to them. So honestly, it was only a matter of time before the damn thing went crazy.

Jamie:

What is going on down there? I've been getting calls all morning from papers asking about my cousin marrying the playboy of the stock car world.

Me:

Good morning to you too, Jamie, and yes, my morning has been amazing (eye roll emoji), and the title belonged to another before him.

Court:

I just want to point out it's not me this time in case anyone has doubts. Well done, Grace, for taking the blame for once; I knew you weren't as good as gold as everyone else thought. You just hide the crazy. Ha ha.

Me:

Court, just you wait. It will be back on you soon enough.

Clint:

Saw the pic, little miss. Really didn't see that one coming, but I'm not hating it. (Winking emoji)

Me:

Guys, it's one big mess. Okay, and before you ask, I'm NOT pregnant!

Clint:

Looks like you got yourself a husband and might I say a fine one at that.

Me:

Clint, you are not helping.

Clint:

Just pointing out the obvious. The man is rough to race; I bet he's just as rough in other places too. Get it girl is all I'm saying.

I can practically hear Jamie growling and Clint laughing all the way in North Carolina with that text message. They may be married, but Jamie is as much of an alpha as you can get when it comes to his love. And Clint is so carefree.

Me:

On that note, I've got to go figure out this mess. I started my new position today, and already, I have to impress our new driver and figure out how I'm to be married to someone I can't stand for two months. Go me! But this has been great. Thanks, guys. Next time, I'll just text my girlfriends. (Face-palm emoji)

Sliding down into my chair, I turn my phone off so that I don't have to watch the damn thing light up with more incoming chats.

Three hours later, the only thing I've managed to do is nothing. Absolutely nothing. Other than staring at my monitor, I've been trying to figure out how I can survive two months acting like I'm in love with the man who turns my insides into mush but also makes me want to throttle him at every turn.

Checking my calendar, I notice that I have a meeting with some of the other **PR** team members get up deciding it's time to head that direction. Opening my door, I come face to face with my new husband, Matt freaking McCall.

"Well, hello, wife," he says in his Southern drawl. "We need to have a little chat." He slowly backs me up into my office. Looking at me like a lion looking as his prey. His sent starting to overwhelm me something like a mixture of pine and racing fuel. Dammit, I shouldn't be turned on by it, but my knees grow a little weak as he stalks even closer to me. Double damn him.

"Quite the mess you seem to have gotten us into with that little stunt of yours last night, Red." He continues to walk me back toward my desk. Granted, the space isn't large, so when my ass hits said desk, I gasp as he steps into my space.

"So, wife, we need to have a little chat." He runs his hand along my skirt and up my waist to hold me in place where my ass has landed on the desk.

Looking up into his blue eyes, I see that fire I love to sass so much. "And what exactly do you want to talk about, husband? I've got a meeting to get to, and you're in my way." Slowly, I try to push away from him.

Brushing the hair back from my face, he stepped closer into my body. "You're mine, Red, for the next two months. I'm going to tease the ever-loving hell out of you. I've watched you strut around with Tinley for far too long after our night together. But pay very close attention; rubbed his hand down this firm chest and toward his jeans, you can't touch this, you're going to have to beg me and then admit you want me before you get anything. You signed up for this, remember that."

Stepping away from me he said. "I'll see you at home, wife. I think you know where it is."

And with that little statement, he turned and walked away, leaving me standing at my desk flustered. Turning to get my papers for the meeting. I let my hands rest on the edge, trying to calm my racing heart.

The rest of the day goes on without a hitch, from my new team-member orientation to meetings about Mila coming into town and getting her settled into her new townhouse. Funnily enough, it's close to Matt. I video-chatted with her just a little to let her know what we needed to do next week. I was more than ready to go home when five o'clock hit. The only issue was that I wasn't going to my apartment. I was going to Matt's house, and my heart sank just a little.

But if he wants a wife, he's going to get one.

Chapter 3
Matt

Today has been the day from hell.

Not only do I have a fake wife, but we're saddled with one another for the next two months. And we need to make the media believe that we're in love and can't keep our hands off one another. The last thing I need is this to blow up in my face and risk my contract renewal. Add in that I have to deal with Mila becoming a part of our team. An I'm beyond stressed at the moment.

It's of course important to bring a female driver on and add her into a male-driven sport. And it's great that Mac wants her to be a part of our boys' club. Mila had been on my radar for a little while. I had watched her come through the ranks of the smaller divisions, so it was only a matter of time before she came up to the big show. Honestly, I'm glad our team snatched her up because she will bring a lot of focus onto us as a unit.

Ugh, running my hands through my hair I think of my wife, Grace. Grace Miller, laughing to myself, she's drop-dead gorgeous, and I know that it won't be a problem showing that we are married outside the walls of my house. That smart mouth is what I'm going to have an issue with. Every time she opens it there is some level of sass that comes with it; And the more she's around me the more I want her on her knees sucking my cock so I don't have to listen to what comes out of it. That may make me sound like an ass, and honestly, I'm okay with that, but the woman just gets under my skin, and I don't know how to break the spell. We had one night, and it has played over in my head since then. It's like she was a siren calling a captain to shore. Shaking my head to try and focus on what I have ahead of me I turn toward the one room that I can have the quiet I need.

Walking into the simulation room, I see all the monitors set up and a single car frame sitting in the center of the room. Taking a deep breath, I walk in slowly. Normally when I come in here to practice for next week's race, it's my one place that I don't have to be on—just me and the screens in front of me. Needing to get focused on the race at hand and block out the shit show that has become my life today. Putting in my specs for the sim, I get to work. Miami is a tough track and one that has always been a pain in my ass. It doesn't matter how much I'm in this machine or on the track, I just can't quite keep it under me. But I'm determined to figure it out this time around come hell or high water.

Two hours—that's how long it took until I was ready to throw my steering wheel at the damn monitor. Frustrated, I decide to call it a day and head home. The only problem is I now have a "wife" in my space when I get there. My place is the one spot where I can just be me; I don't have to put on a show or be this perfect driver. But you know what, to hell with it. She wants to put us in this spot, so she's going to get that version of me. I shouldn't have to act differently. Hell, I may even turn it up a notch just to make her suffer.

Bringing my Charger to life, I decide to make a little stop on the way home. She wants a husband, and she's going to get one. The only difference is I'm not the doting kind. I'm the kind who's going to walk around all day in those gray sweatpants women love so much, and all my shirts will magically disappear. We'll see how she likes that.

"Honey, I'm home," I yell as I throw my keys in the bowl beside the door. I turn on my daily playlist of old country music as soon as I walk in. Granted, that's the one normal thing I'm not going to change. What in the holy hell is that smell? It's like chocolate and a skunk mated and took up shop in my house. Following the smell, I pause just as I get a look at that beautiful peach-shaped ass in the air bent over my oven. Dammit. Nope, I am not going to act on my instinct to go over and smack the hell out of it or bend her over the counter and fuck her for making my house smell this bad. Shaking my head, I watch her for another minute while she sways those gorgeous hips. That's when I notice she has her earbuds in. She hasn't even heard me, so I give her a second to put the hot pan down before I make my presence known. The last thing I need is second-degree burns after she throws that at me. Flashback come of books she launched at my head a few months back—the girl's got an aim I'll giver her that.

"What the hell, Matt?" she yells, turning around to see me staring at her like a creeper.

"What in the fuck have you done to my kitchen, Red?" I say, stepping closer to her. I backed her up to the counter, trapping her in with my arms on both sides of her body. I'm starting to see a pattern when I'm close to this woman—she makes me become a bit of a caveman.

"The last thing I wanted when coming home from my shit of a day is to see my 'wife' turning my kitchen into a war room. What are you making, and why does it smell so bad in here?" I ask, trying to relax just a little to the country music playing in the background.

"Well, husband, if you must know, they're gluten-free choco-late chip cookies."

"Who the fuck would eat those? They smell like ass. Open the damn windows. I don't even think one of those big ass Yankee Candles could fix this smell. It's going to be in the furniture," I say, getting even closer to her.

Blinking up at me, she smirks. "Just so you know, a lot of people are gluten-free, me included, and after the meeting and phone calls with my family today, the only thing I want to do right now is to sit down, eat these cookies, and watch a movie. So if you don't like it, too bad. I suggest you get used to the smell because this isn't the only batch I'm going to make."

Dammit, that sassy mouth again. Running my hand along her neck, I so want to collar her and punish her for what she's done. But I don't; this isn't real, and I need to keep things in check. Watching her reaction, I notice her eyes dilate when I apply a little pressure to her neck. *Yeah, I know you like it rough, Red, but you're going to have to suffer before that happens,* I think to myself. Then I drop my hand. "Clean up the mess, and for the love of God, open a window," I say before walking away. I need a cold shower and some strong will power to get through the next two months.

After my shower, I decide it's time to make her suffer some, so I slip into my sweats—minus underwear and shirt. I make my way out to the living room to find her relaxing on the couch with *The Fast and the Furious movie* on the TV. "Well, what do we have here? A million things on Netflix, and you pick the one movie that I would watch," I say, coming to stand in front of her just so she can look at the goods. And by the slow perusal of my body, I know she's enjoying the view. And just like I thought would happen, the longer she stares, the more my body starts to react. She may have The General coming to the party, but that's all she's going to get. I might be turned on by her, but she can be damn sure that I can hold out.

"See something you like, Red?" I can't help but smirk at her seeing as she's been caught looking a little longer than necessary.

Suddenly, she's clearing her throat, and I can't help but feel good about myself.

"Cowboy, you may have all the right parts that women want, but when you start to talk, it's thrown right out the window," she says, giving me one more look before going back to watching her movie.

"I could say the same thing about you, Red. That gorgeous ass of yours could make any man want you. But it's that sass that keeps them at bay. I'm not sure how that ex of yours stayed with you as long as he did."

Sitting down on the couch beside her, I pick up my phone to order dinner.

"Do you want anything else to eat, or are you going to just eat cookies for dinner?" I ask, trying at least to be nice.

"I'll take a salad from wherever you order from," she says, a little quieter than she was just a few minutes ago.

After getting something to eat, we try to figure out which room Grace might want to put her bags in and whether she wants to grab a few things to make it more homely or if she'll leave it as it is. After watching back-to-back movies, I head to bed. We didn't say much while eating dinner or watching the movies. I didn't want to push it by saying something that she might use against me, so I cleaned up and headed to bed.

Lying in bed, with Grace across the hall, I watch as the fan makes circles above me. I'm a mixture of turned on and irritated with what happened today. Granted, I have this sexy woman in my house, and I need to act like the doting husband for the next two months. But I'm also not able to have her the way I really want. Because that would make things even more complicated than they already are. So I need to stock up on some Vaseline and hit some very cold showers for the next while.

I lie there, mindlessly scrolling my phone trying to take my mind off the spot I've found myself in. Hearing a small knock come from the door. Sitting up some I say, "Come in," as the door opens the woman I both want and hate comes into view. She's wearing a thin nightshirt, showing off those legs, and who the hell knows if she has shorts on underneath?

"Matt, can we talk?" Grace says, all the sass gone from her voice for once.

"Umm, sure, I guess. Can't sleep anyway." I pull myself up to fully sitting up in the bed to get in a better position.

"Listen, I just wanted to apologize for the mess I've gotten us into. I know it's not ideal for you to have a wife. Hell, you don't even keep a girl for a week, let alone longer. But when I saw that woman put something in your drink, I couldn't stand by and watch it happen. I've seen women like her before when I've been out with my cousins, and I don't know, I just didn't want her to use you just to get a story."

"Well, you sure have got us into a situation, Red. That's for damn sure. You know you could have just said I was your boyfriend, and this whole thing would be a non-issue—but you didn't. And let me tell you, I loved getting a phone call from your cousin-in-law earlier today, telling me that I better be on my best behavior or I'll see the turn four wall at the next race sooner rather than later. It was the highlight of my day. So thanks for that."

"Clint called you?" she asks.

Little does she know that I know exactly who her family is and what a shit show this has become for them. I may not be the perfect poster boy of the stock car world, but I've done pretty damn good for myself. The Millers are important. I get it, but I won't stand by and have my life played out in public for all those to think it's a joke.

"Yeah, he did, and granted, the man is downright brutal to race, but he's also one of the nicest people I know outside the car. So to have him tell me I need to toe the line makes me question just what he knows about us, Red," I say, staring at her with as much fire and drive as I've had in a long time.

"If he's got an impression of you off the track, it's from what you put out in the media, not what I've told him. Honestly, my family back home stays out of my love life, and they know that I can't talk about work with them since I'm a part of another team. So other than the weekly catch-up Skype call and our family text group chat, the last thing they heard about my love life was me with Miles, and you know how that turned out." She says.

I look away from her, trying to gather myself before looking back over at her. I know it must be hard coming from the Miller legacy.

"Anyway, I just came to say that I'm sorry about this mess and that I'll make it as easy on you as I can. I have a lot on my plate with Mila coming in, so other than making sure I'm at your side on race weekends, we can just be like ships passing in the night, if that's okay with you, Cowboy," she says, looking down at the floor like there's a math problem on it she's trying to solve.

"Red, look at me. You don't have to feel like a ship. Do you make me angry? Yep, a thousand percent, but I've also seen what a loyal friend you are to those you love. Did I take the news today the way I should have? Maybe not, but it is what it is now, and we can make the best of this fucked-up situation. So let's just take it one day at a time and see what happens. We don't have to be best friends, that's for damn sure, but we also don't have to act like we want to burn the place down when we're in the same area."

Nodding her head, she turns and heads for the door. Slowly closing it behind her, I flop back onto my bed, hands in my hair, pulling at it to feel something other than my heart racing for the beautiful blonde who just left my room. This woman is going to be hard not to grow attached to in the next two months if she keeps coming at me with kind words. I want her sass and those lips on mine. Why can't she just be brutal with me all the time? That way, I won't develop feelings, other than wanting to fuck the life out of her. Throwing the covers off me, I head toward the shower for the second time today—ever since I walked in and saw that round ass bent over my oven. God help me.

Chapter 4
Grace

The door to Matt's room closes behind me. I can't help but wonder why he thought he needed to tell me that Clint had spoken with him. My family has always been one of the things I kept separate when I was in previous relationships. Miles met my cousin, Cortney, once, and that was only because he wanted me to come to a baseball game and knew that Miles was going to be going into the draft. Coming from money and that lifestyle, you never know who you can trust, and honestly, I can count on one hand the people who really know the true me. But with Matt, I want him to know that part of me. I just don't understand why. We've been so cruel to one another over the last few months while Tinley and Ryan found their happily ever after, and it's to keep us both safe from what could have been after our wild night.

Walking back into my bedroom, I notice a small box on my nightstand that wasn't there earlier today when I put my clothes away. I make my way to it and can tell it's a ring box. Matt was in here at some point. Looking around, I pick up the small velvet box, gasping when I see the object inside. The note on top.

"Red, thought you might need some jewelry since you're MINE now."

– Your husband

Opening the ring box, I find a beautiful emerald-cut, dark-green diamond ring with another note attached.

"I looked for a black diamond to match your soul, but it turns out those are special request items, so green will have to do it for now." – Cowboy

I blush at the nickname he signed the note with. Damn, it just got a lot more difficult to not want to be around him.

I pick up my phone and send a picture of the ring to my best friends.

Me:

Well, ladies, it's official, I'm off the market. For a little while anyway.

Tinley:

What the hell? Ryan just filled me in on everything. And damn, girl, that ring is gorgeous.

Mia:

WHAT? I thought you hated that racer. Something about, "he's a fuckboy, and I wouldn't touch him even if he were the last person on earth."

Me:

Well, I may have done something stupid the other day that put me in this spot, so for the next little bit, I'm his wife. (Eye roll emoji)

Lily:

Wait, what have I missed?? I'm over here in baseball land and hear nothing.

Tin:

Grace is married to Matt McCall now. (Laughing emoji)

Lily:

WHAT?

Me:

Yep, it was a ruse that the media took and ran with. Just Google me, it's everywhere.

Mia:

Well, at least his taste in jewelry is amazing. I wouldn't mind one of those.

Lily:

Wow, what a ring! Okay, now that I'm out of shock, are you okay?

Me:

Honestly, I'm not sure, and on the other hand I want to hate everything about him. Then he does something sweet, and I'm like damn him.

Tin:

Maybe y'all don't hate each other as much as you think. Just saying.

Ugh. Lying across my bed, I take a minute to try to figure out if my friends could be right. Maybe we don't hate each other as much as we want. It's more frenemies. Looking back at the ring, I think we can try to make this work for the next two months. Why does he have to make it easy to want to?

Me:

> Well, this has been great, but now I need to try to figure out how to act like I'm in love with my "husband" this weekend in Miami.

After a few more texts back and forth with my girlfriends, I call it a night and try to get some sleep.

The next morning, I wake up and try to get my bearings, then I realize I'm not in my apartment or my own bed. I'm at Matt's house. This is my life now.

After taking a shower, fixing my hair and makeup for the day, and trying to figure out my outfit, I can smell breakfast being made. There's a small smile on my face as I walk out to find a shirtless Matt in gray sweatpants once again. His body is on display for me, not a tattoo in sight, just all smooth skin and tan muscle. Damn, the man is hot, I'll give him that. Clearing my throat, I step into the kitchen, and he turns and notices me with a tiny smirk on his face.

"Morning, Red. Sleep well?"

"Yeah, it was good. Umm, I found this on my nightstand when I went to bed," I say as I put the box on the counter between us.

"Well, Red, you need a ring if this is going to look real," he says matter-of-factly.

"It's beautiful, but I really don't need a ring," I reply as I go to make my coffee.

Grabbing my arm, Matt spins me around to look at him. "Listen to me very closely, Grace," he says, snatching the velvet box off the counter. "For the next two months, you're MINE.

And having a piece of jewelry on your hand will show that to others. I don't share. Just in case you have any ideas." With that, he slides the emerald-green stunner onto my finger.

Looking up at this man, I can't help but smile just a little. I'm his for the next little bit. This may be all for show, but it's a show that I'm going to enjoy. The issue is whether my heart will survive the sudden emotions that I'm feeling.

I move my hand up to his chest. "Well, Cowboy, if I'm yours, then you belong to me. So I better not even hear a small rumble of another woman anywhere near you. Are we clear?" Running my hand down his body once more, I keep my eyes on him, seeing them burn with desire. I reach the band of his sweats and move lower, feeling his erection growing larger the closer I get. His breath hitches just a little as I touch him. With a smirk, I turn and finish my coffee before heading to work, leaving him standing in the kitchen.

"See you tonight, husband," I say as the door closes behind me. I need to get the hell out of Dodge before I drop to my knees as a thank you for the beautiful gift that's now on my left hand.

Chapter 5
Matt

I'm standing in the kitchen, hard as steel after her little show with that damn ring. Why the hell did she have to tease me like that this morning? I'm holding on by a thread, wanting to kiss her, take her, and make her mine in all the ways that I can think of.

The ring was something I thought she needed. I went to a few different shops, looking for the one that reminded me of her. When I saw the green diamond, I knew it was the one. She can act like she hates this arrangement all she wants but that won't stop me from being the husband she needs outside these walls.

Quickly finishing up my omelet and coffee, I head toward my home gym to work out the pent-up feelings that are starting to become more prominent. She's only been here for one day, and she's making it hard not to want her in all the ways I can't have.

I step into the gym and turn the music up to ten, heading for the treadmill. Maybe if I run enough, I'll be able to outrun these feelings.

Eight miles and a million songs later, I'm no closer to kicking this edge. My legs are screaming, and I am soaked in sweat. I've never had an issue getting a woman out of my system before; why is Grace so different? It's because we only had one night, and that one itch is just the tip of the very big iceberg that we've crashed into.

One thing's for damn sure—I cannot fall for my fake wife. No matter what might happen, I don't have time for relationships. I'm trying to bring home a championship for our team. But damn, if I don't want to do everything else with her.

After taking a shower, I head out toward the race shop.

"Well, look who decided to grace us with his presence. Did you have a good night, princess?" I hear Ryan say as I step out of my car, walking faster than needed. But I started my morning off behind, and I'm going to need to play catchup all day. Heading toward the inspection area to check on my car for this weekend, I can feel Ryan hot on my heels.

"Just trying to keep up with you and the little missus is all," I say, laughing as I head toward my stock car.

"Hey, seriously, how did your night go?" Ryan asks.

"Man, are we a bunch of women this morning? Playing gossip on the night before," I say with a little snark.

"Nope, just trying to figure out which one of y'all might kill the other first is all. Tinley and I have a little wager going. She swears that Grace might smother you in your sleep at some point. But I've got more faith in you than that," he says, laughing as we turn the corner, passing crew members and other office personnel headed into work.

"Well, if you must know, I gave her a ring last night. So you can just fuck off," I say, opening the door as we head toward the drivers' office space. "She doesn't want to murder me just yet."

"Jewelry is one way to get a woman on your good side, but you know, if you would both just stop being grumpy toward each other, you might find you're a lot alike. That's all I'm saying," Ryan points out.

"Thanks for the talk, Dr. Know-it-all, but don't you have something else to do today instead of making sure that my 'fake marriage' is up to par?"

"Nope, I'm free as a bird until later, so you're stuck with me," he says, laughing.

"Well, aren't I the lucky one this morning?"

After checking out the car for the weekend and finally getting rid of Ryan, I'm able to get in some sim time before lunch. The tracks we have coming up have always been ones I've done great at. I'm lucky the season is in full swing, and the super speedways are a little way off, so I'm not stressing too hard about that part of the job. The issue I'm going to have before the race is that I have never been one to have a woman on my arm at pre-race events, and I'm not sure how much Grace needs to be in front of the camera to make it look like we're in love and newly married.

Guess it's time to head to see the little missus and figure that out since we work in the same building.

Knocking on her door, I hear her grumble, "Come in." When I step into her office, I can see she has papers all over her desk, and she looks like she's ready to cut someone.

"Hello to you, wife. Just wanted to stop by and talk about some things for the weekend. But honestly, I don't want to be missing a body part when I leave this room. Because you look ready to castrate someone right now," I say, shutting the door behind me and taking a seat across from her desk.

Breathing out a rough breath, I watch her rub her temples as she says, "If you must know, I've been dealing with my father most of the morning, so the only one I want to remove something from right now is him. I have gone over this 'situation' with him so much my head hurts. It's like he couldn't care less about us being married but does about you being a driver."

"Wow, I'm not sure what part of that sentence to be more offended about, Red. I think I'm quite the delight, to be honest," I reply, laughing to myself. "And that ring sitting on your hand looks good." I'm laughing to myself yet again, trying to lighten the mood just a little.

"Did you need something?" she asks.

"I did, princess. We need to plan for the weekend. I need you beside me at all the pre-race events and by the car during the anthem. You've got to be the doting wife all day."

"You do know that I have an actual job here, correct? Like I'm being paid to help get ready for Mila's arrival in the coming weeks," she says with that damn sass that I can't get enough of, waving her hands around her office that looks more like a war room now.

"Yes, Red, I'm aware you have a job. You also have a duty to your husband on race day. Mila is with a different team until the end of the season. So it's not like you'll have to be on her like white on rice. You do realize that, right? This means you can be on me instead." I smirk as I grab a piece of candy out of the bowl she has placed on her desk.

Popping the Jolly Rancher into my mouth, I just sit back and wait for the pushback that is one hundred percent on par with the way the woman is. After what feels like the longest standoff, Grace finally blows out a breath and just nods.

Damn, I really thought I might get more of a fight from her on this. But I guess after the pushback from her dad, the fight is gone for today. And I'm not sure how I feel about that. I love the fire and the sass she brings when talking. This version of her I'm not at all happy with, and it's time I stand up for her. The only problem is she's not really mine, and that might be an overstep for this strong-willed woman. I just need to bide my time and let this play out a little longer but pay attention. If I see this spark disappear one more time, me and daddy dearest will be having words.

Standing up from my chair, I take one more look at this beautiful woman as I head toward her door.

"I'll see you later at home, Red. Try not to be late. I've got some plans for this evening," I say as I close the door before she can protest. And with that, I head toward my car. After the shitty day she's had, I need to show her that I'm not just some playboy —that I can be the good guy.

Chapter 6
Grace

W hat the hell just happened? I can take Matt being cocky, and I enjoy his smart comebacks, but this sweet version? I'm not so sure my emotions can take that. He's supposed to be the playboy, the smooth talker who makes me want to throttle him at every turn.

Granted, my emotions are kind of all over the place with the way the morning has gone. My dad made sure I knew my place and that I don't embarrass the Miller name with this stunt. And that made me feel even more like shit. I spent an hour on the phone with him, trying to make sure he knew that I didn't do this to tarnish the precious Miller name. Of course, my cousins were always in the media more than me, so I'm not sure why he was so worried about it. He finally gave in and hung up the phone. I was so spun out of my zone by the time Matt came in, I had nothing left in me to fight about what he was asking. Yes, the request was simple, to say the least, and I know that Tinley will be at the race this weekend, so I won't be doing this "race walk" alone. She'll be with me, but I still don't like it.

Taking a deep breath, I get back to work. With Matt's words taking up room in my head, I can't help but wonder what the playboy has planned. The more I'm around him, the more I have issues keeping my walls up.

Pulling my thoughts from my "roommate," I check my calendar to see what I have to finish for the day. Call Mila to check in and plan out promo items for the coming weeks with the PR team. I need to get the press packet finalized. It seems like a smooth end of the day.

I have always loved making promo items. It was one of the classes that I looked forward to in college with all the different directions that you could go with one item. Now that I'm working with a certain driver, we have sponsors lined up, and that's part of her brand. I love that I'm getting to introduce Mila to the racing world. Yes, she's been on the racing circuit for a while in the junior levels, but this is going to be her debut to the big show. I'm going to make damn sure that she shows what she's bringing to the table. She isn't just pretty dresses and hair products. She shows that women know about cars and can work on them just like the men in this sport. That's why I pushed so hard to have sponsors that will be versatile. We need to show all those little girls out there who have a passion for racing that you can be fierce, smart, and beautiful all at the same time.

Deep in thought, I don't even realize that it's already way past five by the time my stomach decides to make its presence known. Checking my phone, I have ten missed text messages from the Miller family group chat. Groaning, I know that if I don't make my presence known they'll start calling, but I just don't have the energy today for family. I love them something fierce, but since this whole thing started a few days ago, they have been a lot to take. So I send out a quick response, telling Clint I will see him this weekend, and then I put my phone in my bag, turn off the light, and head toward my car.

Sliding into the driver's seat, I just stare out the window for what feels like an eternity. Although it may have only been a few minutes. I bring my car to life and head toward home.

Pulling up to Matt's townhouse, I finally take a good look at it. Tall windows with dark shutters and a gorgeous, large wooden door that is so inviting that I'm sure it'll be beautifully decorated at Christmas time with the potted trees on either side. It's exquisite, and I was just so aggravated at the situation when I moved in that I didn't take the time to see what I was moving into. I thought it would be some god-awful bachelor pad, but he has a proper home.

Heading up the steps, I unlock the door and am hit with the most amazing smell and soft country music playing over the speakers. I always thought that Matt was a heavy metal or rap fan, but last night, he turned on his favorite station on Alexa and it was old-school country. My heart stops when I make my way into the kitchen and see Matt coming in from the back patio, and I laugh just a little. I see the apron he's wearing, but when I read it, I can't help but laugh. "Kiss the chef or leave my kitchen."

The man doesn't take himself too seriously, and I'm starting to like this version of him the more I'm around him. "Hey, Red. Didn't expect you for at least another hour," he says as he rounds the kitchen to take something out of the oven.

"Well, I figured I better come home when my stomach decides it's done for the day. What smells so amazing?" I ask.

"Ahhh, that's a surprise. Get a shower and put some comfy clothes on while I finish up this, and we can eat," he says, moving me toward the bedroom.

"You know, I'm not sure if I'm in love with this new version of you or just confused with what's happening right now," I say, trying to give him a stern look. But with that apron on, it's hard to keep a straight face.

"Well, it's a good thing you have a few months to find out," he says, coming to stand in front of me, the slow country music playing in the background. Slowly, he pulls me in close just before he says, "Now go shower." Next, he spins me around and smacks my ass to make his point that I'm not needed in the kitchen.

Glancing over my shoulder, I notice that he's already gone back to getting dinner ready, and I head toward the shower to wash this stressful day off.

Thirty minutes and a very hot shower later, I finally make my way back toward the kitchen. The only issue is that Matt is nowhere to be found. The room is dark now. As I look out toward the patio, I find the man in question. He's sitting in his Adirondack chair with a beer in hand, looking out over the lake. When I step out into the beautiful North Carolina night, I'm blown away by the sight in front of me. Lights hang around the small sitting area, and tiki torches are on the perimeter. It makes this one of the most romantic scenes that I've ever experienced. My stomach starts to erupt with the butterflies that I've tried to keep at bay since I first saw Matt all those months ago. Pulling my phone from my leggings, I take a quick picture so that I can remember this moment because it may never happen again. Few men put in the effort like this, let alone for a woman who they aren't dating. But Matt just may be different, who knows?

Just as the flash goes off, Matt turns around, and I'm hit with his beautiful smile, and there's that single dimple. I'm sure only a few people get to experience this smile because you can tell this is his real one, not the one that's made for the cameras on race day or for his fans.

"Hey, Red, ready to eat?" he asks just so casually and without a care in the world. I love that he can be so relaxed while I'm over here having an internal freakout. I'm trying not to have it written all over my face so that he doesn't ask a ton of questions.

I must stand staring at him for longer than I should because he comes up in front of me.

Pulling me into his space, he tilts my head up to look into his ice-blue eyes. "Grace, you can look all you want. Hell, I know I have. But just so we're clear," he says before grabbing my hand and trailing it down his hot-as-sin body, "this is off limits until you can admit that you want it as bad as I do." His Southern accent comes out more when he's teasing me, and I kind of love it. "Now come, sit down, and eat." He completely throws me off balance with that comment.

His gruff laugh pulls me from my lust bubble as I make my

way toward the table he set up. If he wants to play it that way, well then, game on, Mr. McCall.

"So, tell me what smells so good, Cowboy."

"Well, I decided to make you roasted chicken with vegetables since I know you can't have fried food, which I learned the other day after you made those god-awful cookies," he says with a smirk. Secretly I knew he loved those cookies because the next day they were all gone, and I didn't eat all of them.

After sitting down and pouring my glass of wine, I go to tell him thank you for cooking, when my stomach decides it's then it needs to make the most unladylike noise. It makes both of us laugh, breaking the thick tension that had started to build since we sat down.

Dinner was amazing; the man can cook. I'll give him that. "So who taught you to cook?" I ask.

"My mom. All Southern moms think they need to teach everyone. So as early as I can remember, she had me and my brother in the kitchen, learning how to do everyday things. I think at one point, her words were, 'No sons of mine won't be able to cook, clean, and take care of themselves. It's not up to the wife to do everything. You need to share the responsibility with your significant other, not have them be the only one to cook and do the daily chores. She will be your other half, not your house-keeper or your mamma'," he says in an extra-thick Southern accent that makes me laugh because I can see the small yet fierce Southern lady, giving her sons a lesson and not taking any lip from them in return.

I love that. A lot of guys nowadays have no clue—it's how they were brought up, or it's just the circles that I've always been a part of. If every momma raised her sons with this attitude, men would be men and not stay boys.

"Remind me to thank your mom next time she's at a race. She really deserves a medal for making you a decent human being, even if you are a fuckboy."

"Was—past tense, Red. I *was* a fuckboy. Don't forget that I'm a married man now," he says, throwing his left hand in the air, and I notice he's now wearing a ring too. How had I not noticed that in my office earlier? Oh, that's right, because I was so wrapped up in my own shit, I didn't even notice his hand.

Standing from the table, I grab my wine and head toward the Adirondack chairs near the fire where Matt was sitting when I came out onto the patio earlier, and I sit down. I can see the stars so clearly as it was a peaceful night, looking out over the lake. The stars are one thing that I love watching since I moved to North Carolina to attend school. Having grown up in the city, they were one thing that I could never see. I always loved it when we went on vacation outside the busy city life as kids because it meant I could just play out on a beach and look at the stars glowing in the night sky. Lost in my love of the stars, I didn't notice Matt coming to sit beside me.

"What are you thinking, Red?" he asks, his voice so low.

"Just trying to figure you out, honestly," I reply, feeling my walls coming down just a little bit. I don't know if it was the wine or just that I'm finally becoming comfortable with him, but it's making me want to open up, even just a little. I know that I can't trust myself to be completely open and honest, but we could come to a point where we might be frenemies instead of enemies. Only time will tell, I guess.

"I'm an open book, honey. You ask, and I'll answer. I've got nothing to hide, and I'm sure you've Googled me at some point. Hell, our best friends have been together for what seems like forever, so we might as well get used to being around one another. You can only hate me for so long before you'll have to love me," he says with a smile, making that dimple come out once again.

"Wow, you really think a lot of yourself, Mr. McCall, don't you? That all women just want to throw themselves at you and never look back."

"Haven't had any complaints so far, darlin', and I always give them more than a good time," he says with a smirk.

Damn him and that smile. My mind is instantly taken back to when we were together all those months ago, and I'm trying my best not to let him see the effect he has on me when he mentions that wild night.

"Red, it's okay to think about me when you get yourself off tonight. I know I sure as hell will be thinking of you," he says as he rises from his chair to clean up dinner.

Slamming my head back against the chair, I stare up at the stars once again. Only this time, I'm not relaxed like before, I'm turned on, and fuck if that doesn't make me want him even more. But I will not give in. This little chess match just went into a new arena, and guess what? I'm about to up the ante.

Chapter 7
Matt

Cleaning up the kitchen after dinner, I wait to see what Grace will do with the little statement I made before walking away from her, leaving her sitting in the chair. I knew that she had been turned on. I could tell by the way she looked at me. Those beautiful eyes grew wider, and her lips opened to say something, but it never came out.

The conversation at dinner was easy, but the second it turned into talking about my fuckboy past, I could tell I'd hit and triggered a reaction. She might play the hardass like I don't matter to her, but her body tells me another story.

"Thank you for dinner. I think I'm going to head to bed," I hear her say as she walks toward her room.

"Night, Red. Sleep well," I say over my shoulder, cleaning the remaining dishes and putting them away.

"Night," I hear her say as she quietly pads across the hallway toward her room.

Just as I put the final dish away, my phone pings from the counter.

Ryan:

How did the missus like dinner?

Looking down at the message, I can't help but laugh. Who would have ever guessed a year ago we would be here?

Me:

Well, let's just say she was surprised I could cook. (Laughing emoji)

Ryan:

Maybe if you play your cards right, she'll want a little dessert.

Me:

(eye roll emoji) She left me washing dishes and headed to bed.

Ryan:

Then you did something wrong because Tinley thinks that should have worked.

Me:

What? I did what y'all said would get her attention.

Ryan:

She's the one playing hard to get.

Me:

Wow, so insightful. Thanks for that.

Ryan:

You're welcome. (Laughing emoji)

Me: Night, man. You have been so helpful with this text—NOT.

Putting my phone on silent so as not to disturb me, I head in the direction of my bedroom. When I turn down the hall, I hear the faintest of moans coming from the feisty blonde's room. I can't help but stand in front of her door, knowing I'm a complete creeper, yet I can't seem to make my feet move forward when her moans get louder, and then there's the slightest buzzing noise.

Standing closer to her door, I think to myself, *she's in her bed, pleasuring herself,* and that makes me so hard. I have thought about Grace since the second I laid eyes on her, and now she's in my home, in my personal space, and her scent is everywhere I turn.

Listening to those beautiful moans coming from the other side of the door is becoming pure torture. Before I can even think about what I'm doing, I open the door ever so quietly.

The room is in utter darkness, and she's so focused on getting off that she doesn't hear me open the door. As I walk toward the bed, she must finally sense me because she slows her pace on her beautiful pussy. She's completely bare before me, and I am left staring at my fake wife, wanting to fuck her so hard that no man will ever compare to me. Because for two months, she's mine, but we're riding a fine line on letting each other in.

"Keep touching yourself, Red, I know you're wet for me. I can smell your arousal from here. Are you thinking of my dick while you use your toy? How my cock knows just how to make your body sing in the best way, and that you want me, even if you might hate me."

Another moan comes from her as I continue to watch her work herself up again.

"Are you just going to stand there watching me?" she asks breathlessly.

"I like the view I have right now, Red."

I'm mesmerized by how smooth her skin is, how her breathing becomes more rapid as she moves her hand up her gorgeous tits, palming her nipple and pulling just enough to make my mouth water. I try to rearrange my dick but it's pointless. It's hard as steel, and the only way I'll get any relief is from her tight cunt, but I want her begging me first. I want her to want this as much as I have for the last few months.

Unable to take anymore, I walk closer to her but stay just out of reach. She turns up the speed on her little friend and moans even more. Unbuttoning my jeans, I slowly unzip them, drawing her attention to my movement.

"What's wrong, Red? Cat got your tongue?" I ask as I push my jeans down my legs just as my cock springs forward.

With our eyes locked, I slowly begin to wrap my hand around my dick. Precum leaks from the tip as I stroke myself while she moans, watching me. She gets faster with her vibrator, and it has me on the verge of coming just from this simple act.

This woman has me under her spell and doesn't even know it.

"Tell me what you're thinking, Grace."

"That I want you to fuck me," she says without hesitation.

Chapter 8
Grace

If you told me a month ago I'd be lying in bed on the verge of getting myself off while Matt stands beside me, stroking himself, I would have laughed you all the way into the new year, but here I am. This gorgeous specimen of a man and that cock are perfect for me. Yet he's made it clear that I can only have it once I tell him what I feel for him. Because he knows it's not just a one-sided attraction. And with how wet I am right now, I know it's not.

"Fuck me, Matt. Make me come so hard that I'll walk differently tomorrow," I say, staring at his cock as another moan comes from me. The vibrator's getting me so close to my release that I pull away, not wanting this connection to be over just yet.

He inches closer to me, his cock lining up with my mouth as I lick my lips, wanting to taste him. He strokes himself a few more times, then just as I think he might do as I ask, he stops, drops his hand from that beautiful cock, and reaches down for his pants.

Sitting up abruptly on the bed, I glare at him.

"What the fuck are you doing?" I ask, biting back at him.

"I told you, Red, I'm not fucking you until you admit you want this as badly as I do. And that includes your amazing lips wrapped around me," he says just as he turns and walks from my room, closing the door behind him.

Watching him close the door, I am left beyond unsatisfied. I know my vibrator isn't going to do it tonight. Damn this man and his fucking body. Why the hell did it have to be him that I was stupid enough to play house with? The one man my heart and head have been at war with for the last week. Granted, if I'm honest with myself, who I've wanted since our time in his hauler all those months ago.

I lie there for a few more minutes, letting the day run rampant in my head. Coming home from a long day at work to find this beautiful Adonis of a man cooking supper for us, to having easy conversation, then seeing him stroke himself in front of me. Ugh, this day. Maybe if I soak in the tub for a little bit, I'll be able to calm down and reach the release I so desperately need.

As the water turns cold, I pull myself out of the tub and dry off. I'm still on edge when I slather my lavender lotion on. I will not give Matt the satisfaction of knowing that the only way I'm getting off is with him either in my head or in my body for that matter. With a huff, I snuggle under my comforter to try to sleep, but it's going to be a long freaking night of tossing and turning.

I wake up in a shitty mood, which was not how I expected my morning to go when I had that Greek god of a man standing in front of me last night. Getting dressed a little too aggressively this morning, my new bottle of perfume goes flying from my hand and onto the floor, breaking as it hits the tiles. I can't fucking concentrate on anything besides images of Matt's dick in front of my face last night. Grabbing towels to try to get the mess cleaned up, I'm on my hands and knees when my phone buzzes. Looking up, I see that I have a text from Tinley.

> Tinley:
>
> Hi, lady. How was your dinner last night?

I finish cleaning up the perfume bottle before I reach for my phone to reply to the message.

> Me:

The food was great; the afters could have been better.

Tinley:

What did he do?

Me:

It's what he didn't do.

Tinley:

Wow, I didn't see that coming.

Me:

Well, I didn't get to come at all. Now I'm pissed off and have just dropped my bottle of perfume all over the bathroom floor.

Tinley:

Did he do anything?

Me:

Oh yes, he did just enough to edge me, then backed up and left me wanting him. Freaking asshole.

Tinley:

Ha ha, sorry, girl, but that sounds like a you move. You may have met your match.

Me:

You aren't helping, Tin.

Tinley:

> Sorry. So what's your next move?

> Me:

> I've got some ideas, but I may just save them for the track this weekend. (Winking emoji)

> Tinley:

> I can't wait to see what you come up with.

Putting my phone on the bed, I finish getting ready. I only have one more workday before we head to the racetrack for our first official event as a couple.

Boarding the Mac Motorsports plane the following morning is tense, at least for me it is. I avoided Matt most of yesterday, but I know that's going to be a lost cause now that we're meant to be playing the part of a loving couple. Only our close friends and management know the truth, so the next three days in Miami are going to be interesting.

"Grace!" I hear Tinley shout as I make my way to her.

"Hey, Tin. Hey, Ryan. Fancy seeing you here," I say, trying to make light of this entire situation.

"Hey, Grace, how are you?" Ryan asks.

"I'm fine, thank you for asking."

"Hello, wife," Matt says with that slow Southern drawl, pinning my back to his front as he slowly moves his hands down my waist, directing me to our seats across the aisle from Tinley and Ryan.

Turning to face Matt, I see the slight smirk on his face. He knows that I've been avoiding him, and this weekend is going to be a game of cat and mouse.

Slowly, I look up at him, running my hand up his hard planes and around his neck. I pull him close so that only he can hear. To anyone looking on, you'd think we're getting ready to kiss, but what I want to do is chop his beautiful dick right off for what he did to me the other night.

"Hello, dear husband. Is that right hand sore today? Do you need more Vaseline? Because from the way you left me the other night, you'll be needing lots of it for a while. I hope you have a great memory," I say before kissing him so hard that a moan comes from his mouth, and he's hard within an instant. I pull away and make sure to wipe the red lipstick off his beautiful lips and then sit down in my seat for the flight to Miami.

Chapter 9
Matt

Looking down at Grace, I rearrange myself in front of her, wiping my mouth with my thumb to get the remainder of the dark red off my lips. Well played, wife.

Once I take my seat beside her, I can't help but smile. If I get to kiss Grace all weekend, I'm damn lucky, and even if they might be a little hate-filled, that was still one of the hottest kisses I've ever had.

The flight to Miami is quiet with the occasional conversation with Ryan about the race, and the PR team briefs us on what events we have to attend as soon as we land.

When the pilot says we're landing, I'm so ready to get off this plane. I thought that I'd be the one making Grace uncomfortable on this flight, but it was all her.

Leaning over my lap, she calls out to Tinley. "Tin, want to come over to our hauler when we get to the track? I need some help picking out my attire," she says, rubbing her tempting breasts over my ever-growing erection.

Pulling her back up and placing her in her seat, I turn to face her. "Red, rub your tits on me again, and I'll throw you over my lap for the rest of the journey and give you that spanking I know you want so badly."

It's one thing to sit beside Grace before we had rings on our fingers, and another to sit with her and want to join the mile-high club the whole ride.

I stand up once the pilot has said we can leave the plane, I hold my hand out. "Time to go, wife."

"Thank you, husband," she says with a smirk.

Following Ryan and Tinley out to our waiting car, I keep Grace close to me. The media may not be at the airport, but I want her to know that I will protect her from the storm that's coming.

"I saw the list of events for the weekend. Do they normally have you going from start to finish each day? Seems like a lot. Do you have any downtime to get ready for the race?" Grace finally asks once we're in the car and headed toward the track.

"Yes, it's not as bad as it looks on paper. Insignificant things here and there, and you don't have to worry, you only need to be at the major stuff. You can spend time together with Tinley in the trailers until that time."

The ride from the airport to the track is quiet; the closer we get the more Grace shuts down on me. I knew that this might be overwhelming for her, but I wasn't expecting her to pull away. She's from this world but I guess being the one in charge is different from being the one front and center.

"Hey, Red." I put my hand on her now bouncing knee to try to ease her fears of being in front of the upcoming crowds. "Look at me, Grace." Slowly she turns to face me, and her eyes are so wide. My confident wife looks like a deer ready to run at the first sound of a gunshot.

Not knowing what to say that'll make her feel more relaxed, I do the one thing that I've wanted to do for days. But I've kept my distance so we didn't cross a line that I don't want to cross with her, because I want her to want it as much as I do.

Cupping her face in my hands, I slowly bring my lips to hers. Those beautiful plump lips that I've been wanting for so long. I push my tongue against her mouth, hoping she'll open for me, and she does, slowly. Finally, she relaxes, melting into the kiss. Tasting her, I can't help but want to deepen our kiss as we head toward my hauler. With the blacked-out windows in our car, spectators can't see us, so I don't have to worry about pictures. Gently pulling back from our kiss, I whisper, "Are you okay?" I want to check on her before we get out of the car.

Quietly, she replies, "Yeah, I think so, just a little overwhelmed with the situation that I've put us in. I guess it's finally hitting me."

"Don't worry, it's going to be easy. It's not like you hate me that much, Red," I say with a smirk before catching her lips one final time and opening the car door. "Stay there. I'll come and open the door for you."

Walking around the front of the car, I open the door for Grace, and taking her hand in mine, we walk toward my hauler. Luckily, spectators and photographers aren't allowed back here, so we can come and go as we want. Having her hand in mine feels like the most natural thing on the planet. This weekend might just be fun.

"So, Red, this is my home away from home." Looking up at my hauler, I'm transported back to the one night we had in here months ago. I'd had a shit race, and she was getting over heartbreak. Who would have thought months later that the media would think we were married and she would be by my side?

"Cowboy, don't get any ideas just because I'm here this weekend." Heading into my hauler, to put her bag away.

"I'm gonna shower quick before I head to the garage to check in with the team about the car. Make yourself at home. What's mine is yours anyway, right?"

Taking the world's quickest shower, I pull on my jeans and T-shirt along with my boots. I walk into the living space to find Grace asleep on the couch. The woman is so naturally beautiful it takes my breath away when I see her. Reaching down, I place a small kiss on her head, whispering that I'll be back later, and then make my way to the garage.

Stepping out of my hauler I feel my head switch to Matt

McCall racer and not Matt McCall the person, lets get this weekend underway.

"Well, well, look what the cat dragged in," I hear as I walk toward my car in the garage bay.

"Did you think I'd show up late, Doug?" I ask, looking at my crew chief. Doug's a good guy, and I know he's been biding his time this week to give me shit. It's just a matter of time before he'll come out of the gate about it.

Laughing at me, he turns around to get back to setting up the car for the practice we have in a few hours. "Just figured the little misses would have you tied to the bed from the way you hauled her to your trailer so fast when we arrived. I came by and saw you helping her out of the car. I figured I didn't want to interrupt the newlyweds. Congrats, by the way. I didn't even know you were dating, let alone married. Seems like that's something you might clue me in on. You know, since we're together every week," he prods with a shrug and a look that tells me he knows I'm so full of shit and that it's not really a marriage.

"Yes, well, it happened fast, honestly," I say, walking over to my car to get in and make sure the seat is ready for later today.

Doug walks over to my car and leans over the window so only I can hear. "Listen, bud. If it's real, that's great. I don't really know Grace, but I've heard of her family. You could have done worse. And if it's not real, then you're a damn good actor because I see the way you look at that woman, and you better be careful," he says, slapping my roof and walking away, leaving me staring at the steering wheel.

Practice was a bitch and a half. After all the sim time I spent on this track this week, I still wasn't able to get it under me, and by the time we finished our laps, I was more pissed at myself for not being able to get the car where I wanted it. Every time I thought I was getting it going in the right direction, I hit a rough spot on the track, and I was back at square one.

Pulling back into the garage when the black flag flew, I was more than ready to get out of the car and just go to relax for the night. Turning the corner to pull into our garage I'm met with the stormy eyes of my now wife. I hadn't made it back to the hauler after I left her asleep earlier today. But I think I'm glad I didn't from the way she's looking at me right now. I'm not sure if she's pissed at me or something else.

Climbing out of my car, I'm met with those eyes again. Only, when she comes over to me, the next thing I know is she's got me pressed against the car door and her lips are on mine before I even get my bearings on what the hell is going on.

"Hello, husband," she purrs at me, pulling away from our kiss.

"Hello, wife," I say in return. "Miss me?"

"Well, you did leave me all alone today, so I thought you might need a little something when I finally got my hands on you," she says with a smirk.

Leaning in close so only she can hear, I whisper, "I told you, Red, that if you want me, all you have to do is admit it, and I'll have you under me so fast that you won't know what hit you." I kiss the side of her neck as I pull away. Smacking her ass, I walk away toward Doug to talk to him before leaving the garage for the day.

Dammit, why the hell does he have to make it sound so simple? Do I want his hands all over me? I'd be stupid to say no. But I also don't know if I want to open that can of worms because the last thing I need to do is catch feelings for my husband. It's just temporary, and less than two months from now, we are going to go our separate ways, and my dad will be happy that the Miller name wasn't made into the laughingstock of the racing world.

"If it isn't Mrs. McCall." I hear the one voice that I had been avoiding all day.

And this is why I stayed at the trailer longer than I should have. I just didn't want to see Clint.

"You do realize you can't avoid me or your cousin the whole weekend, right? I mean, come on, lady, I'm a big deal around here," Clint says with a laugh, walking up to me and wrapping me in a hug.

"Ugh, you have got to be kidding me. You found out my grand plan," I say with a laugh.

"How was practice?" I want to change the topic before he starts asking the million and one questions that I know are on the tip of his tongue. My cousins may not have found me yet to ask, but Clint is the nosy one, and he can spot a lie a mile away.

"Ha, don't you even try that shit with me, Grace; you know just how practice was. You may not have been in the pit box watching your 'husband,'"—*yep, he used the quotations on me when saying husband*—"but I know you saw I was leading the pack, as always," he says, crossing his arms on his chest.

"Ugh, fine. Yes, I saw." I may not be a part of Miller Racing, but it's still a part of me. Mac Motorsports may be my employer, but Miller is my home, my safe space, and I will always want the best for them. Granted, the lines are blurred right now with Matt being my husband.

Bracing for the impact I know is coming, I finally look at Clint and say the one thing he was waiting to hear. "Fine, well, my husband is waiting for me to go to dinner." I hardly get the sentence out of my mouth when Matt rounds the car and comes to stand beside me.

Placing his arm over my shoulder, he looks at Clint, and it's like they're having some alpha exchange with one another that only they know about. I want to roll my eyes so hard that they'd get stuck in the back of my skull. Just when I'm ready to walk away from them, they burst into a huge fit of laughter.

"How's it going, Clint? Your car was on point out there today," Matt says, going to shake his hand as he holds onto me like I'm going to run away at the slightest jest.

"Hey, Matt, you know you can't mess with excellence, and I get up and piss excellence every day. One day you might be able to catch up," Clint says with a smirk.

"Grace, I got to go, or Jamie is gonna be pissed if I miss another dinner because I'm wandering around the garage area. I'll text you later because I still have questions, and I'm sure you'd love to tell me all about pretty boy here instead of Jamie or Cortney," he says, laughing as he turns and heads to where I can only guess Jamie is waiting.

"Ready to head to the hauler and find something for supper, wife?" Matt asks, grabbing my hand in his as we head out.

Chapter 10
Matt

R ace day in Miami comes early on Sunday morning, and I'm more nervous about the race today than I have been in a long time. I had tied my race shoes four times, and I couldn't get my hands to work right. Trying to shake off the nerves that may have something to do with the blonde bombshell standing beside me as the national anthem plays, or it could have something to do with all the extra attention that I have on me now that I'm married to Grace Miller. Over the course of the weekend, word began to spread as to who Grace is and the power that comes in the racing community with the Miller name.

I was asked more questions about my personal life this weekend than I care to admit. Granted, up until a week ago, I was the fun-time guy, or as Grace pointed out, just the fuckboy of the racing world. But I've never been asked who I was dating or anything personal. It's always been focused on my racing career, so I sure as hell am not a fan of the love life stuff.

The sounds of the crowds and the flashes came as we walk toward my car, my hand in Grace's as we now stand, listening to the singer belt out the anthem. Just looking over at this gorgeous woman has me finally starting to relax. This woman is mine. For the next two months, she's all mine.

As the national anthem ends and I start to get into my car, I turn back to see Grace with tears in her eyes as she stares at me.

Bracing my hands on either side of her face, I'm blown away

that I get to see this side of her. I haven't known her for very long, and when we did talk, we didn't go too deep because, well, she hated me, and honestly, I didn't want to know more. But I want to get to know all about her the more I'm around her, and I want to be the one she trusts with her heart.

"Give me a kiss, Red. I've got to go to work and kick Clint's ass out there," I say with a slight laugh to try to get a smile out of her.

Leaning into me, she presses those red lips to mine, and my heart rate picks up. Yeah, we may be putting on a show for the cameras and those watching, but if that's what I need to endure to have these full lips on mine, then dammit, that's just what's going to happen.

"Good luck out there, Cowboy, and give 'em hell, okay!" she says, pulling away from me, making sure that I don't have any lipstick left on my lips as I get into my car and start to strap in for three hundred laps.

One hundred and fifty laps down. We're halfway, and I have driven the hell out of my car today. The changes we made on Friday were for the better because the car is just where I want it.

"Clint's coming up quick on you, Matt. Watch your back quarter panel," my crew chief, Doug, says through the headset.

"I see him. Is Ryan around to block?" I ask to look for my teammate so that I can have a little cushion in case he comes on me faster than I expect.

"Ryan's coming, but he may not get to you before Clint. You better get ready to hold him off on your own." Doug's voice comes through my headset.

Coming out of turn two, I see Clint's car coming up fast. I'm in fourth position, and if I keep up my pace, I could pull off the win. The only problem would be him. He's one hell of a racer and always makes it impossible to pass if he ever gets around you.

"On your right, Matt," my spotter calls as I see Clint make his move to go.

When I started in this sport, I was always told that I was a levelheaded racer, and I prided myself on that. My teammate, Ryan, is the opposite of me when he gets into the car. He turns into the devil and doesn't give two shits who he takes out.

Just as we round turn four and head to the flag, I feel my car shake. Shit, am I cutting a tire down? That's about right, of course; we wouldn't be at the end of a stage and something would go wrong so that we don't lose laps. Slowing to the bottom apron so that I can get to the pit row, I radio that the tire's going down and I'm coming in.

Twenty laps—that's how long it takes me to get back to the top ten. The pit stop took longer than I wanted, and I made sure that my pit crew knew I was not happy. I had to put the pedal down and get back into the mix. Clint ran away from the pack with Ryan hot on his heels. I'm going for that top spot, and I'm not stopping until I'm in it.

I bob and weave through the top ten as the laps tick by. My spotter keeps me aware of what lines seem to be running the fastest, and it helps put me in the top five with fifty laps to go. It gives me the boost I need to get to the back bumper of my teammate.

I turn my radio to the station that connects me to Ryan just for a little bit of fun.

"Hey, bud, guess what?" I say, making sure that Ryan sees me in his mirror.

"Matt, now is not the time for your silly shit. I'm trying to win," he grits out, sounding a little irritated that I've come on his radio.

"Just wanted to say, watch this," I say just as we come out of turn four, and I slingshot around him. Ryan is one of the few racers who, if you can get around him, will give you the line, knowing that you earned it. Granted, he's my partner in crime, so we always give the other some grace. Except when it comes to winning, then it's game on, and the best man would come out. Yet he knows that I have the better car today and is willing to let the pass happen.

Coming up into the second position I set my sights on the first place car. Now it's just Clint that stands in my way.

For twenty laps, we go back and forth with each other. Just when I think I have the line, he weaves and leaves me a few car lengths behind. I know that my car is faster. I had my car chief track his lap times for the last ten laps, and I had him, coming off the corners. I just need to find the line and blow past him. The only issue I have is I'm running out of laps. Less than ten to go, and I'm still following behind him. I'm not above wrecking someone if they push, and honestly, the longer we play this cat and mouse, the more frustrated I'm growing.

Three laps to go, and I know it's now or never to get around him. Pulling out of the line, I start to go, but he cuts down in front, shutting me out again. Laying back just a hair, I wait, and just when he starts to come down again, I dart up the lane and get around him, coming out of turn two. Kicking the car into the next gear, I start toward the white flag.

Just as I cross over the start-finish line, I hear Doug come over the headset. "Wreck coming out of turn four. Slow it down."

Shit, now we're going to have a green-white-checker. Normally I don't mind them, but Clint has been a bitch to pass. I'm going to run the chance of him getting back in front again, and I won't have nearly enough laps to pass him. I need to be ready to punch it as soon as that green flag drops.

"Ryan's gonna line up behind you, and hopefully, he can give you the boost you need to get out in front of him. So be ready," Doug calls.

Coming up to the start line, Doug comes over the radio once again.

"Go, go, go. Green, green."

With each gear change, my adrenaline spikes a little higher, and I know that if I'm going to win, it's going to be now. So I throw it into another gear and block Clint. Getting out in front of him, I make it back to the line as the white flag goes. Four turns, that's all. The one track that I've wanted to conquer and there are only two turns left. I see Clint, trying to keep Ryan behind him, and I know that it's mine. One turn, seeing the checkered flag coming down as I cross the line. *I did it*, I think, gripping the steering wheel a little tighter just as I started to relax.

Chapter 11
Grace

I sat on top of the pit box, watching my husband win at Miami. The weather was perfect today. It was a little breezy, so I didn't have to worry about wearing a ton of clothes. He had battled Clint most of the race, and when the tire issue came, I wasn't sure he was going to make it back to the top spot, but he proved to everyone that he had the car to beat.

Just as I step down from the pit box, I hear my name being called. Turning, I see my best friend, Tinley, running toward me.

"Grace, I'm so happy for you guys. I know Matt's wanted to win here for a while, and look at that—you may just be his lucky charm," she says while taking my hand and walking us toward Victory Lane, with more pep in her step then I was expecting from my once wallflower friend.

Walking down the pit lane, I feel eyes on me and see the flashes from cameras going off, and just as I think I might get away without having to give a statement, a female reporter comes up. Not wanting to be rude, I say hello, just as she pushes the recorder into my face.

"So tell me, Grace, what's it like watching your husband battle your family's race team for the win?"

Stopping to take a deep breath, I put on my PR hat and give the answer that's easiest.

"Well, Marcy, I love my family, and I'm happy when they do well, but when it comes to my husband, I always want him in

Victory Lane over anyone else. So if you'll excuse me, that's where I need to get to," I say as sweetly as possible, grabbing hold of Tinley again and making my way to congratulate Matt.

Victory Lane is one place that I never thought I'd be as a girl-friend, or for me right now, as a wife. I grew up around this, and I had no interest in drivers. So to find myself now celebrating as the doting wife, it's all so weird. I watch Matt's car come to a stop in the middle of Victory Lane, the smell of rubber in the air and the motor blowing smoke as he turns the car off. I can't help but smile at him, and his smile covers his face from inside his helmet. He wanted this win so badly; I could hear it in his voice over the headset. And when they had the green-white-checker, he had to work twice as hard to keep Clint at bay. He deserves the win; he worked his ass off, and I'm so happy for him.

"Go to him, Grace. It may be fake, but I know he wants you beside him when he gets out of that car," Tinley says quietly as she pushes me toward him.

Walking over to Matt, I can't help but feel butterflies in my stomach as he pulls his helmet off and climbs out of the car. Covered in sweat, the man is still a walking wet dream. He may piss me off and get under my skin but damn, my "husband" is hot.

Pulling me to him, he smiles that genuine smile at me.

"Looks like I have a new lucky charm, Red," he says as he leans down and kisses me quickly just as the crew members spray us with Gatorade.

Looking up at him, I can't help but laugh and hug him tight.

"I'm proud of you, Cowboy. Now go celebrate with the team. I'm gonna stand over there with Tinley," I say, starting to walk away, only to be pulled back into his chest and thrown over his shoulder as we make our way up on stage.

"Put me down, you caveman," I say, laughing as we go to meet the crew members.

"I think I kind of like this view, Red. If we weren't on TV

right now, I might just smack your ass, but I wouldn't want to give your dad any extra reasons to hate me more than he already does," Matt says, setting me down on my feet just as Ryan comes over to congratulate him.

"Talk about making an impression, bud," Ryan says, slapping Matt on the back and doing one of those guy side hugs. "Next time, just take her in front of everyone and claim her." Ryan laughs as he comes over to me and gives me a hug too.

"Have you, by any chance, seen my other half, Grace?" Ryan asks.

Pointing over to the corner, I guide him to where Tinley stands, talking with a lady in a NASCAR official uniform.

Ryan and Tinley are so sickly sweet it makes my teeth hurt. The moment she connects with his eyes, she smiles so big I can't help but feel just a little jealous, thinking that I want someone to look at me the same way she does him. With so much love he'd take on the entire world. And for Tinley, he did.

After two hours of interviews and hat swaps with different sponsors, we are finally able to head back to the trailer. I am exhausted, walking next to Matt, leaning into his body. If I'm this tired, I know that Matt must be dead on his feet. Stepping into the trailer, Matt grabs the back of my neck, spinning me around to face him.

"Thank you for today, Grace. Having you standing with me may have been the kick in the ass I needed to prove to myself that I deserve this life," he says, crowding me against the wall as we step into the bedroom.

"I didn't do anything, Cowboy; I was just there. That was all you," I say, running my hand down his chest. He's still sticky from the Gatorade bath, and I notice his eyes don't leave mine. Seeing what I might do next.

"So tell me, Cowboy, what do you usually do after a win?" I ask, knowing the answer but wanting it to come from his lips.

"Well, it depends on the win. Sometimes, I go out with the

team, and we just relax. Other times, I'm so wired up that I need a release and look for a willing participant," he says with a smirk.

Looking up at his face, I can't help but want to drop to my knees and congratulate him on the win today, but something holds me back. Maybe it's the fact that I shouldn't cross this invisible line, or maybe it's because I can feel my heart starting to become involved, and I'm not sure I'm willing to give it away again.

As if he can sense my dilemma, he takes my face in his hands and kisses me. Slowly at first, then his hands start to wander down my back and grip my ass, lifting me off the ground, and on instinct, my legs wrap around him. My mind is screaming to stop but my lady bits have another idea altogether, especially since he left me on the edge earlier this week. Unable to stop myself, I grind on his already hard dick, loving that I have him so turned on just from our kissing.

Chapter 12
Matt

Winning at Miami may have just become my favorite win in my career. Seeing Grace in Victory Lane talking with Tinley, I don't know that I've ever been filled with this much joy before. Yeah, I know she's playing the part of my wife, but sometimes when she looks at me, I think things may be shifting some with her.

We may have started out as enemies when this arrangement began, but in the last week, being close to her, I've seen her walls slowly coming down. It may be at a glacial pace, but it is happening. I know that if I wanted her in my bed right now, it would be so easy. The problem is, I told myself when this all started that she would be begging me before I went there again.

Pulling back from Grace, I enjoy seeing her eyes glaze over with lust and the way she grinds on my dick right now. I don't want to take it from her, but she's going to see who's in charge, and it's not her.

"Tell me what you want, Red," I say, gripping her ass harder, making her gasp at the movement.

"All you have to do is tell me you want me as much as I want you, and I'll strip you bare right here and fuck you like I know your needy pussy wants," I whisper in her ear, sending goosebumps along her skin.

"Now, what will it be?" I pull back more from her, looking

into those beautiful eyes to see what she wants. But for some reason, this sassy, smart-mouthed woman can't get her words out.

Setting her feet on the ground, I take a step back. I let out a frustrated growl, turn, and walk toward the back of the bathroom.

It's going to be a long-ass cold shower for me tonight it looks like. Pulling the door open to the bathroom, I turn the water on. I'm standing under the spray when I hear the door to the shower open. Unable to turn around and look at her, I leave my head bowed and brace my hands on the wall as the water pelts me around my shoulders.

Slowly, she wraps her arms around my middle, and I tense under her touch. Unsure of what she wants. I'm in my head, trying to figure it out, and I can't see straight. I'm freaking falling under her spell even more the longer we spend time together, and she has turned into a siren from a Greek story, calling me to her.

"What are you doing, Red?" I finally ask.

"Let me take care of you, Cowboy. I want to show you how you make me feel. I may not be able to say it because it scares the hell out of me now, but I can show you," she says as she begins to stroke my aching dick.

"Red," I groan as she picks up the pace. "Shit, what are you doing to me?"

Turning to face her, I push her against the shower wall. She gasps as I cup her breast, needing to feel her under my touch. I wrap my other hand around her throat, forcing her to look at me.

"You are driving me out of my fucking mind, Red. One minute you want me to fuck you, and the next you pull away and can't run fast enough to get away from me. Well, guess what? I'm done playing your fucked-up games, and it's my turn to show you who's in charge."

Her eyes darken, and I know that I've said just what she wants to hear. She's been pushing me for a reason. She's been the one who's been in power, and I didn't even know it until now.

"What are you waiting for, Cowboy? I've been thinking of all dirty was you can ruin me since you climbed out of that car in Victory Lane," she says with a smile that I fall for every time she's near.

"You want me, Matt. I can tell how bad you do. The question is are you gonna punish me, or are you gonna be a good boy?" she says before I cut her off so she can't finish her sentence.

"On your knees now, Red. You are gonna show me just how much you want this before I fuck your tight cunt."

With the water hitting my back, she does as she's told and then wraps those beautiful lips around my cock.

"Shit, Red. Damn." Grabbing her hair in my hand, I start to slowly fuck her mouth. If she wants to play the part of the sweet and innocent, then I can play the part of the villain.

"That's it, Red. Take my dick like a good girl for me. Show me that you want to be fucked once you get me off. And you better swallow every bit of it."

I can feel myself getting close. Grace defintly knows just what she's doing. I'm definitely not going to last if she keeps up this pace. Then when she looks up at me with those beautiful eyes, I come with so much force I see stars.

"Damn, Red," I say, pulling her to her feet as she licks the cum off the side of her mouth. Kissing her, I can't help but taste myself on her, and that turns me on.

Stepping out of the shower, I dry us off and head toward the bedroom. Tossing her onto the bed, I'm on her faster than I can think. I need to be inside her, and my dick got the memo too.

"Play with yourself, Red. I wanna see what's mine for tonight." Dropping her legs open, she begins to play with her clit. Damn, she is gorgeous.

"Are you wet for me, Red?" I ask, stroking myself while I watch her.

"Yes, Matt. I am so wet for you. Please fuck me," she finally says.

That's all I need to hear, and I'm on her quicker than my best qualifying time. Pushing her legs apart, I lick her clit. Desperate to taste her and make her come on my tongue first.

God, she tastes good. Like honey and sin, all mixed into one. If I died today, I would be happy having been between her legs. Picking up my pace, I insert one finger into her tight pussy and curl it as I eat her even more.

"Tell me, Red, how should I fuck you tonight?" Taking her sweet clit back into my mouth, I bite down softly as a moan comes from her. Licking and moving my finger fast, I start to feel her come apart in my mouth and let her ride out her orgasm. Pulling away, I bite the inside of her thigh. Marking her.

"Roll over, Grace. I'm gonna fuck you from behind. I can't be gentle with you right now, and I don't think that's the kind of man you really want," I say as I slap her beautiful ass while she wiggles it at me.

Looking over her shoulder, she gives me that sassy mouth that gets me so hard.

"You just going to stare at me, sir, or are you gonna fuck me?"

Lining my cock up with her, I thrust into her tight cunt, letting out a growl as I bottom out in her. Gripping her hair, I pull her toward me so that I can fuck her just how she asked for it. She wants to be my dirty girl, so that's the game we'll play.

Thrusting into her hard, she cries out my name, spurring me on. I smack her beautiful ass, wanting to leave a mark so that tomorrow she'll have the reminder that I claimed her and that I'm the only one she wants.

Getting close to my release, I flip her over so that I can come all over her beautiful tits. Then she'll know who she belongs to. Pinching her clit, she climaxes on my dick so hard I almost come, but I pull out at the last minute, sweat dripping, and my balls tighten before I'm painting her with my cum.

Once I'm empty, I sign my name on her chest, then get up

from the bed, leaving her lying with my cum on her beautiful chest.

"Think you can hand me a washcloth, Cowboy? You know, since you made a mess on me," she says with a small laugh.

Walking over to the bed, I grab her hand and lead her into the shower so this time we can clean off and get ready for bed.

After washing my cum off her and then wrapping her in a towel, we head back to the bed, and I think she might have a freak-out moment, but it never comes. She grabs one of my T-shirts, pulls the covers back, and lies down ready for bed.

Lying in bed flipping channels on the TV, I think she's fallen asleep when she rolls over to face me.

"Matt."

"Yes." Answering her, I roll to face her in the bed.

"I just wanted you to know that I was so proud of you today, and the way you raced Clint, you could have easily taken him out at any point, but you didn't. You deserved to win," she says so softly that I wonder if she's awake.

Bringing her close to me, I wrap my arms around her, kissing the top of her head.

"Thank you. That means more to me than you could know. Some think being a clean racer isn't the best tactic, but that's always been my style. I think of it as if I can pass them without wrecking anyone for the win, then I deserve it. I don't need to resort to nasty driving just to win."

Looking up at me, her eyes are heavy, and I kiss her gently.

"Get some sleep, Grace. We have to be up shortly to catch the flight back to Charlotte," I say, kissing her one more time before seeing her eyes close, and then her breathing evens out.

Chapter 13
Grace

Waking up the next morning, I can't help but have a smile on my face. Last night was unexpected but in the best way possible. Matt may have given me just what I wanted, but I gave him even more.

Getting up from the bed, I find my clothes for the flight home and get dressed. Walking into the small kitchen area to see Matt reading something on his iPad with a scowl on his face.

Grabbing a cup off the counter and fixing my coffee, I make my way over to where he sits, still with a look of disgust on his face.

"You know if you keep looking like that your face is gonna be like that permanently," I say, sitting down across from him.

Looking up, he pushes the iPad to me so that I can see what has him scowling this early in the morning. A newspaper article that claims our marriage is a joke is trending online, and I can't help but laugh when I read it.

"Did Matt McCall marry Grace Miller just to make a name for himself in NASCAR or is it the real deal, guess time will tell?" the headline reads.

Skimming the article—its so obvious it's a fluff piece, one used to get clicks on the internet. Literally none of it makes sense, and you can tell someone pulled all this from their ass.

"Matt, you have got to be kidding me. This is what's causing

93

that gorgeous face of yours to scowl this morning. You're joking, right?" Pushing my coffee away, I get up to stand beside him.

Grabbing his face, I pull him to look at me.

"Cowboy, this story is nothing. Did you read it? It's false. If you want the real one out there, then we need to tell it. When we get home, make a joint statement on our new joint Instagram page. That way, people get it from us and not from what they think they might know."

Leaning down, I kiss him, wanting to deepen the kiss so that he can tell that my emotions are starting to come into play as we get closer. Last night changed things between us. The only problem is, am I willing to give this playboy my entire heart? Pulling away from our kiss, I look into his beautiful eyes. "Come on, we need to get to the plane before it leaves without us."

Walking out to the waiting car, Matt follows behind me. I can tell that the article has really rattled him. Granted, I get that a lot is on the line for him this season. He needs to do great and keep his head down. That's why the next two months are so important, especially with his contract at Mac coming up for renewal and the season finishing up.

I think to myself that the press is going to come and go but it's what you turn it into that sticks with people. And being in PR, that's just what I'm going to do. They want a love story, well then, we are going to give them one for the ages.

As we make our way up the steps of the jet, I smile as I see Tinley and Ryan already in their seats, ready to leave. Tinley raises her dark eyebrow at me as I sit down across from her. The girl has this natural ability to see when something is different. Most times, I'm the one to give her shit about things, but I know it's time for the tables to turn.

I feel a blush come across my face and neck. I can't face my best friend now. But I can feel her eyes on me. Just as Matt comes to sit beside me, my phone dings.

Tin:

Well, if this isn't the walk of shame, I don't know what is. (Winking emoji)

Me:

Don't know what you're talking about. (Laughing emoji)

Tin:

Oh, Mrs. McCall, you had a lot of fun last night after that win. Don't worry, once we get in the air, we'll be having a talk because I want details.

Me:

(face-palm emoji)

Tin:

And great job hiding that mark on your neck. (Laughing emoji)

Pulling my camera mode up on my phone, I search my neck to see what she's talking about, and sure as fuck, he left a mark on me for all the world to see. I was so focused on that article this morning that I forgot to check my neck and cover up this bite that I knew was there last night.

Hearing her laugh beside me, I can't help but give her a WTF look. I know she's enjoying this a little too much.

I smack Matt in the arm and turn to him.

"Ouch, what the hell, woman? What did I do now?"

"Have you seen my fucking neck; it looks like a lion mauled me!"

"Not my fault this lion wanted to mark what's his," he says, coming close to my ear, making goosebumps run along my arm.

"Ugh, you are such a cave dweller." I turn to face him. "You mark my neck again, and I'll castrate you where you stand. I have a job where I'm in front of major people daily. I do not need to cover up marks on my neck each day."

"Wife, you're mine, and I'll mark you every day to keep others away if that's what it takes to make them see that."

Rolling my eyes, I lean back in my chair as the flight attendants come over the intercom. They tell us we're getting ready to take off.

Chapter 14
Matt

Sitting next to Grace on the flight has been quiet. Which was fine with me. I was still reeling from the article about our marriage. Yes, it was someone just wanting to get some information out there on us. And it was complete crap, but it still made me see red when I made the stupid mistake of reading what the internet trolls had commented.

- Looks like Playboy finally leveled up with that hottie.

- Does she even realize what she's gotten into with that one?

- Well, he's got a sugar mamma now. The Millers are
   rolling in money.

- Damn, that's one hot couple. Too bad it looks like they
   want to kill each other.

I've never had to deal with my name being thrust into the light with such force before. Yeah, I've been in NASCAR for a while now, and I've built a steady career while at Mac Motorsports, and the press has always been pretty good to me, especially when they latched onto my friendship with Ryan. They gave us that stupid nickname a while ago with Shake and Bake, and I didn't even mind that. But now, they're putting Grace on display, and I don't like it one bit. She didn't sign up to be picked apart just because she's attached to me. So I'm going to protect her at all costs and make sure that they know I'm not after the Miller name.

Pulling up to our townhouse, I'm so tense by the time we get home I can feel it coming off me in waves. I know that I need to put a little distance between myself and Grace so that I don't take out my anger on her because she doesn't deserve it.

I slam the trunk closed on my car, grab the luggage, and head inside with Grace following behind me.

"Wanna tell me what's going on, Matt? You look like you're going to explode at any moment," she asks, concern written all over her face.

Walking into the bedroom to put my suitcase down, I turn to face her. I inhale a deep breath, counting to five and then releasing it.

"I just need a little bit of space. The article this morning has me in a weird headspace, and I'm not sure how to process it."

"I have an idea. Do you trust me?"

Going to stand in front of her, I wrap my hands around her waist. To think, when we started this little arrangement, she wanted nothing to do with me. But after last night, I can tell she's changing and seeing that I may just be what she needs too.

"Red, I've trusted you from the moment you stepped foot in my house."

"Okay then, come on. We're gonna have a little fun today."

Watching her walk toward my dresser, I wonder what she has in mind for the day. It's a little later in the afternoon, so the sun is blazing down.

After a few minutes of looking in each of the drawers, she finally pulls out what she's looking for. Throwing it at me, I catch it, wondering what she's doing.

"Put that on and meet me down by the dock," she says, looking back over her shoulder and leaving me standing with a pair of swim trunks in my hand.

Ten minutes later, I'm standing by my boat, waiting on Grace. I love being out on the water about as much as I love being behind the wheel of a race car. Did she know that? I don't remember telling her that wakeboarding is one thing I do to relax.

Looking up, I see Grace coming down the backyard toward the deck. Damn, the woman gets hotter every time I lay eyes on her. She's carrying a bag as big as her, and even with the cover up, I can see her hot-pink bikini underneath. Rushing over to her to grab the bag, I can't help but sweep her in my arms and kiss her.

"Damn, Red, I don't know what you have planned, but I'm already in a better mood just from seeing that smile on your face," I say, pulling away and taking her bag.

Laughing, she moves toward the boat.

"Let's go, Cowboy. We are gonna have a lazy lake day," she says, climbing onto the boat.

Following her, I put the bag beside her and made my way to the driver's seat. Backing the boat out of the dock, we head out onto the water.

Lake Norman has always been a place I love; it was one of the selling points of my house because of the dock. I like to take my boat out as much as possible during our off weekends, which isn't as much as I like. Before Ryan was attached at the hip to Tinley, we made it a weekly thing to come out on the lake and wakeboard. We used it as one of our workout days since it takes a lot of your core muscles to stay up on the board.

Looking over at Grace, she's removed her cover and is resting back on the bench seat, soaking up the sun in her pink bikini, her sunglasses covering her eyes. God, she's gorgeous, and then seeing the marks I left on her last night has my dick standing at attention. She hasn't even bothered to cover them up, knowing it's just us. Pulling out my phone, I snap a quick picture, knowing that it's going to be my new screensaver. Then I get the idea to show the world my wife, so I decide to post the picture to my Instagram feed for the world to see my sexy woman.

@MattMcCall24
"Love seeing my wife so relaxed on the lake" #LuckyMan.

After I post the picture of Grace, I follow the path to a small alcove that I found last summer. I know it'll be perfect for a little private time. Slowing down along the alcove, she notices the boat has stopped moving and pulls her sunglasses up.

"Why did we stop?" she asks.

Approaching her, I lean over.

"Are you trying to torture me, woman?" I ask, my voice coming out a little more gruff than normal.

"I don't know what you're talking about, Cowboy. I'm just getting some sun while you drive me around, and hopefully, that foul mood of yours will go away," she says with the level of sass that she knows makes me crazy.

Grabbing her around the neck, I draw a gasp from her.

"You know what you're doing, doll, and if you wanna play that game, then I'll be glad to punish you," I tell her.

Rolling her eyes at me, I can't help but be turned on even more with the sass that comes from her.

I pull her onto my lap so that she can see just what she's doing to me. I push her bikini bottoms to the side and run my finger over her clit, feeling how wet she is for me.

"So wet for me, Red. Looks like you want me to punish you. You get even wetter when I'm rough. You know that, right?" I tell her as I start to tease her, feeling her start to move her hips as my hand plays with her even more.

"Tell me, Red, you want me to fuck you right here where anyone can see? You like the idea of someone watching you get railed so hard that you scream my name?" Bringing my lips to her neck and kissing that spot that she loves so much, I make her shudder.

Grinding against me, she just moans as I insert two fingers into her hot pussy.

"Yes, Cowboy, don't stop," she moans.

I move to kiss her and pick up the pace. "Damn, you're so wet for me, Red."

Pinching her clit, I feel her moan into our kiss, and I get even harder.

"Take my cock out, Red. I need to be inside you." Sitting with her in my lap, I could fuck her in this position, and even if someone came by, she'd be covered. Luckily, the lake is quiet today and the alcove I pulled into is away from the main area. The last thing I need is for someone to take a picture of me fucking her from behind, which is what I really want to do right now with her in this little bikini.

Undoing my swim trunks, she stands just enough to pull them down, and my cock springs free. I pull her bikini bottoms to the side once more, and she slowly lowers herself onto me.

"Woman, if you don't hurry up and sit on my dick, I'm gonna fuck you for all to see, no matter if there are cameras around or not," I growl at her as she slams down on me, making us both moan. Causing an echo around the alcove, the beautiful surroundings and fresh air are lit up even more with this beautiful woman on my lap. Burying my face in her neck, I nip at her ear, and she's more glorious than any setting that I could be in.

Rolling her hips, she slowly drives me to the point of coming, then pulls back. I'm so turned on by her, I know it won't take long, but damn, I didn't think I was going to be like a teenager when it came to her.

Grabbing her neck once again, since she loves that and wants the rough side of me, I thrust up into her hard a few more times before I feel her orgasm come as she clamps around my cock. It sends a shock wave up my spine, my balls draw up, and my jaw clenches. Even with the blinding sun coming down on us, I'm seeing stars as this beautiful woman relaxes into my chest.

Once we come down from our orgasm glow, I sit her back on the bench and rearrange myself so that I can get up to find something to clean her up. I reach into the bag she brought and find some towels. Reaching down to wipe the cum that was dripping down her thighs, I can't help but smile at the sight.

"Cowboy, I know you like seeing what's yours, but can I have that, so I can clean this mess up?" she says with a smirk.

"Red, you have no idea how hot that is," I say, handing her the towel as I make my way back to the driver's seat so that we can explore the lake a little more.

Walking over to me, she places her arms around my neck.

"You know, if you told me a few months or even a few weeks ago that I would be here with you, actually enjoying your company, I would have told you that you'd lost your mind, Cowboy, but you're growing on me," she says, coming to sit on my lap as I slowly move around the lake.

Kissing her lightly, I laugh at the turn of events over the last few days.

This amazing woman is finally opening up to me, and I'm not planning on wasting any time, making her see that this might just be worth the risk to both our hearts.

"What's so funny, big man?" she says, pulling away from me to stand.

I smile as I look up at her and say, "Just thinking that I'm a lucky SOB for you putting that ring on my finger as a joke. Because now you're stuck with me."

Chapter 15
Grace

Standing next to Matt, I'm flushing at the way he talks to me. I never in my life would have thought when I met this man those months ago that I would be falling for him, yet here I am. I could tell this afternoon when we got back that he was stressed out, so I thought spending some time on the lake would be good for him. And after the orgasm that he just gave me, it's been even better for me.

"All righty, Cowboy, time for you to have a little fun."

"If you think that what we just did wasn't fun then there is something wrong with you. And I'll need to have my way with you again," he replies, coming to stand and wrapping his arms around my waist.

Playfully swatting his chest at his comment, I move around him to the captain's chair.

"Whoa, whoa. What is happening right now, Red?" he says, looking at me like I just grew three heads when I start the boat up.

"Sit that ass of yours down. Let me drive this bad boy."

"You sure you can manage it, baby?"

"Oh, I can manage it. Why don't you get your wakeboard out and have some fun?"

Once he's settled on his board in the water, I yell out, "Hang on, Cowboy."

Gunning the boat to pull him out of the water, I watch in the mirror as he gets up and starts to move over the lake. He makes so much effort that it makes my heart soar even more. Shaking my head to clear my mind, I feel like my emotions are all over the place. The man has me falling for him. Trying to keep him at arm's length for so long is futile. He may have been the fuckboy of the racing world, but in the brief time I've been with him, I've seen him changing.

We race down the lake, and Matt jumps waves with the biggest smile. I can see he's finally relaxing. It's reassuring that today was just what he needed. Slowing down, I watch as he sinks into the water before releasing his board and climbing back into the boat.

Watching the water fall down his amazing body, I just stop and stare at him. I can hear him clear his throat, so I look up and see he's smiling that genuine smile only I see, and dammit, I blush.

"Wanna try, Red?"

Unable to control myself, I burst out into a fit of laughter.

"Did I say something funny?"

"Matt, there are a few things you need to learn about me. One, I'm not into any type of sports activities. And two, I will never know what to learn. I'm more the 'sit on the sidelines and cheer those who are doing it' girl." I walk over to the co-captain's chair and take a seat as Matt moves toward the captain's chair, and we head back toward the house.

With the wind hitting my face as we race toward the house, I look over to the man whom I once loathed and realize that my ice heart may just be changing, and it scares the living hell out of me.

Chapter 16
Matt

Today has been one of those core-memory days that will go into a special Grace Box. I finally relaxed and didn't have a care in the world. The media can step on a Lego barefoot for all I care, and it is all because of her. She saw how stressed out I was with that article and took it upon herself to do the one thing that I didn't even think she knew I enjoyed aside from racing. Being on the water is the one place I don't have to be on all the time.

Stepping up to the house and opening the door, I let Grace go ahead of me, and my phone pings. I look down to see Ryan calling.

"Hey, man. What's up?" I ask.

"Hey, Tinley wants to know if you and Grace want to go out for dinner. She's been trying to reach her, but she hasn't answered. She was starting to freak out when I said I'd call you."

"Hang on, let me ask the little missus."

"Grace, Ryan wants to know if we want to meet them for dinner tonight. Said Tin's been trying to get a hold of you."

"Yeah, I saw my text messages from her," she says, laughing, then she appears back in the living room after changing out of her bikini.

"Sure, we can go. I guess I owe her a drink since she was freaking out with me not responding."

"Yes, man, we can go. Meet you in about an hour at the burger place around the corner." Hanging up the phone, I head toward the bedroom to get changed so I can take my girl to dinner.

Walking into the restaurant an hour later, I see Ryan and Tinley already at a table out on the patio, away from everyone else.

"Hey, thanks for grabbing a table. Sorry, it took us a little longer than we said. Someone just couldn't get enough of this body," I tell them, smirking as we sit down.

Grace's face turns a light shade of pink, and it's fast becoming one of my favorite things. I noticed that she only blushes when we're in public. In private, she's a lioness with me.

I scan the menu for what I'm in the mood for, and my phone vibrates in my pocket. Reaching to see who texted me, I'm puzzled as to who it could be, considering the one person I talk to daily is sitting across from me.

Clint:

Good job on the win last night. See your balls finally dropped and you came out swinging. (Laughing emoji)

Me:

Thanks, man. Guess I just needed some motivation, and Grace did just that.

I'm laughing at myself as I wait for the reply to come from Clint.

Clint:

Also, saw your IG post. You know she's
going to kill you when she sees it, and if
you're replying now, she's not received
that notification yet.

Me:

Got to show off what's MINE to the world.
Especially since the press think
otherwise.

Clint:

As long as you're good to her, then you
have my blessing. Jamie & Cort are
getting on board too since I told them
you're a stand-up guy. Don't make me
regret it.

Clint:

Tell Grace to text me later. She's coming
up to Boston next week to see her dad.

Me:

Will do. Have a good week.

Clint:

You too. See you next weekend, and I'll
beat your ass this time. (Laughing emoji)

I'm looking down at my phone, thinking about what Clint texted. Grace hasn't mentioned that she's going to Boston next week to see her dad. This draws out my anger, but I'm not even sure I have the right to be angry about it. Granted, we haven't talked much about anything since we crossed the line after my win this weekend. After getting home and then spending the day relaxing on the boat, we just haven't talked. Now we're having dinner with Ryan and Tinley. But once we get home, I'm going to find out what's going on and why her dad's summoned her home while I would be out of town.

We finally order our food, and I enjoy catching up with Ryan, but I'm on edge. The more I think about the idea of her going to Boston, the more it doesn't sit well. I don't know her dad, but just from the way she acted after only one phone call with the man, I wonder if he's always accustomed to getting what he wants. I've known Jamie and Clint for a while now, and they are good people, and the more time I'm with Grace, the more I see that behind that sassy mouth, she's got a big heart. I'm chipping away at it slowly, but I can see it there.

We pay the bill, say goodbye to Ryan and Tinley, and head back home. We don't live far from the restaurant, so we decided to walk. The North Carolina air is just perfect. The breeze coming off the water makes it have a light chill in the air, showing that fall might just be here soon and my days of wakeboarding after a race weekend are ending.

She was quiet on the walk back home and headed straight to her room as soon as we walked in the door. Knowing that we have a few items to talk about, I make my way to her room. I knock softly and wait for her to call out before I enter.

"Hey, I was just getting ready for bed. What's up?" she asks before she picks up my T-shirt and heads toward the bathroom to brush her teeth and change out of the flowy dress she wore to dinner.

"Come on out here, Red. We need to talk."

Peeking her head out of the bathroom, she sees me standing in the middle of her room, hands in my pockets. I've never been a serious guy, but I can turn it on when I need to, and right now, that's what I'm going to have to do.

"Ummmm okay, what's up, Matt? You're kind of freaking me out a little, I gotta say." She comes to sit on the side of her bed.

"Heard some interesting information tonight via text from Clint, and I need some clarification on some things." I go to sit beside her on the bed, making sure to put some distance between us so that I'm not tempted to grab her and put her on my lap. Because since yesterday, that's where I want her at every waking moment. Right next to me.

"Okay, what did he have to say?"

"He just pointed out to me that while I am gone next week, instead of you being with me, you'll be in Boston with your dad. Care to explain that?"

Chapter 17
Grace

What the hell is happening right now? My family have decided they need to make Matt aware of my plans to go up to Boston and talk with my dad and explain what's really going on. Reginald Miller is a man who you don't just call up on the phone and tell your great ideas to. Nope, he is the man who you schedule an appointment with so that he takes you seriously.

Looking at Matt, I do feel a little guilty for not telling him, but after the weekend that we had, I honestly forgot about it.

"Who told you that?" I ask.

"I'll give you one guess, but I'm sure you don't even need it. But you *do* need to tell me what's going on. I thought we were in this together. Yet you're keeping this from me," Matt says, a little more aggressively than I care for. Which makes my claws come out. I don't even want to wait for him to tell me why he's acting like a dick right now.

"Okay. Listen to me very carefully then.

"One—I don't have to tell you my every waking move. Let's make that clear right now. Fake marriage or not.

"Two—I'm going to see my father and attend a fundraiser for my cousin while I'm there. You're gone for a long stretch that weekend, so I figured it would be as good a time as any.

"So if you think you have some claim over me because of this weekend, then you, Cowboy, are mistaken. It's gonna take more than a few orgasms to make me bend that easily. I've spent my whole life being told where to be and how to dress. Until I came to North Carolina, I wasn't even able to go out without someone following behind me to make sure I was safe. So you, my husband, can back up about five steps."

"Woman, all I asked was whether you're going to Boston. I said nothing about making you bend to my will or controlling you. And I damn sure ain't going to start treating you like some mafia princess when you leave the house. I'm a good ole boy from NASCAR for hell's sake. But I do think I deserve to know that you're going up there," he replies after I've finished my rant.

Sitting on my bed, I stare down at my hands. Yes, Matt is right—he did deserve to know that I won't be at his race. But I just couldn't find the words to tell him that over the last few days.

Playing with my beautiful ring, it makes me smile a little as I look over at Matt. He's trying to be so serious and in control, but I can see the man who I'm falling for breaking free the longer we sit in silence. I know that all I need to do is use my power of persuasion on him if I want to get what I want. But did I want to play that card on this or save it for another day?

Looking over at him once more, I decide to be an adult and have the conversation. Which I both love and hate since I know that we're making progress in our "I don't know what." Friendship? Fake Marriage? Who the hell really knows because we've blurred the damn line, and I'm starting to be okay with it.

I take a deep breath and turn to face him.

"Matt, I know that I should have done this differently, but honestly, I didn't want you to have to endure my father. You think I'm scary. Ha ha, who do you think taught me? I can tell you for damn sure, it wasn't my mother; she's as sweet as they come. She makes my teeth hurt."

"I know you feel like you need to do everything alone, and I get it, really I do. Hell, you're the one who decided to put this in motion by putting a ring on my finger. But I don't want you to feel like I'm not with you," he says.

"Cowboy, that may be the sweetest thing you could say, but this is something I need to do for myself—by myself. I need to explain to him exactly what's going on and why. He doesn't need to read any more papers and make judgments about me, and especially not about you.

"It's a quick trip. I'll meet with him on Friday, and then my cousin, Cort, is having a fundraiser for his baseball team. He's the GM for now because he's retired and living with Dylan and her sweet baby." I can't help but laugh at that to myself. I would never have dreamed that Cort would have ended up with the life he has now, but he couldn't be happier, and the family that he has around him and his kid is amazing.

"Next time you think it's a great idea to keep things from me, just remember that I'm not the enemy, okay? That's all I ask," he utters, reaching over to kiss my forehead before pulling away and walking toward the door. "Your dad may think that you've embarrassed the family name with this stunt, but just know right now that I will always be on your side no matter what."

Well hell, just when I think he's going to go all freak-out mode, he does the most swoon-worthy thing with that forehead kiss. Damn him.

Standing up and going back to the bathroom, I finish getting ready for bed. I pull on one of Matt's shirts, and those butterflies are back in my stomach once again. I think I may be falling for my fake husband. The only problem is, am I willing to risk my heart with someone who I'm not even sure could give me his in return?

Walking to my bed, I go to pull the comforter back but come to a stop when Matt appears in my doorway in nothing but those damn gray sweatpants that he wears so well, showing off those deep V lines that make me weak.

"Red, don't even think about sleeping in that bed anymore. First thing in the morning you're bringing all your stuff into my room from here on out," he states in his husky Southern voice, making those butterflies appear once again.

Looking at him, I bring out the sass because, let's face it, the man loves that more than the sweet version of me that I was today.

"Is that right, sir?" I purr, putting my hand on my hips and bunching his shirt up so that he can see I have some of the smallest panties that I could find on. I thought about wearing none, but then thought this might be funnier in case he came back to my room. And I'm glad I did.

"Red." He growls my nickname and comes to stand in front of me.

"Get that gorgeous ass to my room now." He gives me one more chance to go willingly before I know he'll go all cave dweller and carry me.

I peck him quickly on the cheek and sway my hips more than I would normally as I head out of my bedroom and into his.

I call over my shoulder as I get to his room, "You coming, Cowboy, or are you just going to stand in there with your dick hard as a rock for me?" I giggle to myself when he comes charging into the bedroom, throwing me onto the bed.

Chapter 18
Matt

The week has gone by quickly, preparing for the upcoming race weekend and the long stretch we have ahead of us, leading up to the final four races. Our team is close to making the final four, and this win last weekend brought us closer to that number-four spot.

"Matt, you look like you have a fucking hanger in your mouth, man. I know you've been getting sexy regularly since Grace finally gave in, but damn, man, even I'm a little jealous," Ryan remarks, coming to sit beside me as I finish up looking over paperwork for this weekend.

"Well, I'll have you know, bud, this is my normal face. You just don't get it during the week as much. But hell, Grace does make me smile more, especially when I can make a special trip to her office."

"Dude, I do not need to know that!"

"Let's just say, you may wanna knock before entering her office anytime soon is all." I'm laughing as I get up to go.

I leave Ryan sitting by the desk as I finish up the inspection with my team and make sure that my seat is ready for the road course this weekend. The setup is always a little different for road courses than ovals, so I like to sit in the car and make sure that I'm comfortable with the position before I load it on the hauler.

Living in North Carolina, the haulers are already being packed to the brim for the next two weeks because of the long stretch we have at the end of the season. And being across the country, they had to load the road course car and then the Texas car. That will make for a long two weeks, but luckily, being a driver, I have the option to come home in between. And I would want that if Grace was going to be home, but next week, she'll be in Boston while I'm in Texas.

Thinking about that kind of makes me wonder what our life might be like if we really made a go of this. I know she has a job here at Mac, and next season she'll be traveling with Mila each week, so I'll see her each weekend, which would be ideal if she wanted to be with me after these two months. Guess that's one thing that I'll decide in less than a couple of months now.

After packing all the items into the front of the hauler that I want on this trip, I head down to Grace's office to check on her.

"Okay, great, Mila. I'm so excited to see you next week, and thank you for coming to the fundraiser with me. I know that Cort will appreciate it," I hear her say as I walk into her office, shutting the door behind me.

"Glad I'm able to come and not have a race that weekend. It worked out perfectly. I mean, how could I turn you down? Think any of those Boston Revs will be there for me to stare at?" Mila questions with a playful tone in her voice.

Coming around the other side of the desk, I'm compelled to kiss the top of Grace's head, and I smile at Mila on the screen in front of me.

"What's up, Mi? Causing trouble in the small show this week?" I ask.

"I'll have you know, Matt, I have been very ladylike this week. Thank you very much," she fires right back before she and Grace both break out into a fit of laughter.

"Yes, from the way you two just started laughing, I'm not so sure it's a good idea for y'all to be paired up next week while I'm all the way in Texas."

Grace looks up at me with those beautiful eyes of hers and kisses my lips softly.

"Cowboy, I can shop all day, but I know where I buy my groceries," she says in a sultry voice that has me wanting to bend her over this desk right now.

"Yeah, on that note, I'm not. Grace, I'll call you next week. Unless you have anything else for me this week," Mila shoots with a smirk as she hangs up the Skype call.

Spinning Grace around, I finally get to kiss her just how I've been wanting to since I left her this morning.

Moaning into our kiss, I know I need to back away, or I really am going to bend her over this desk. The big guys upstairs definitely won't like that and might give me a ding on the contract negotiations.

"You almost finished for the day, Red? I'm headed out but wanted to check in with you before I leave."

"No, I've got about three more hours of work before I'm done," she says with a sigh.

"Well, just let me know when you're on the way home then, and I can just order us some takeout."

"Sounds great," she says before giving me one last kiss as I walk out of her office.

Closing the door behind me, I smack right into Ryan.

"Shit, man, are you trying to give me a heart attack today? I'm gonna start putting a damn bell on you. Freaking hell, for as big as you are, you shouldn't be able to sneak up on me that easily," I chide.

"If you weren't in that Grace bubble, you would have heard me, shithead," Ryan says.

Pinching the bridge of my nose, I start to walk toward where my car is parked.

"Ryan, why are you following me, man? You're like a dog with a bone right now. You know that, right?" I'm laughing at my friend because it's true that this guy has turned into a golden retriever instead of the aggressive dog he used to be.

"Just seeing what you're up to. I'm bored, and Tinley..." he starts to say.

"There it is. Tinley's busy, and you have no one to play with, ha. So that's why you're up my shit today. I knew something was going on with you but couldn't put my finger on it."

"Hey man, that's not fair. You're my best friend," he starts to say.

"Yes, so you say. But what happens when Tinley calls and you drop me? If I make time for us to have a guy hang out, you're not going to bail on me then, right?"

"Not me and you, Shake and Bake, bud," he replies.

"For the love of God, don't call us that. That dumbass name finally died down. Let's not bring it back into the light." Laughing, we continue to head toward our cars.

"Okay, bud, but the first text or call from your little lady and guy day is over," I say, getting into my car and heading toward Ryan's place. I sent Grace a quick text to tell her I'll be back later. Damn, I really am starting to be a whipped man.

Ryan's condo has always been my place to come to relax. We'd play video games, drink beer, and eat pizza. I haven't been to his place since Tinley moved in, wanting to give them space. Yet the minute I step foot into the doorway, I can tell a woman lives here now.

"Ummmm, Ryan, did Martha Stewart explode in your house? What the hell happened here?"

"Well, Tinley made some changes, but don't worry, the gaming system is still in the living room. I made sure that stayed."

"For the love of all things holy, please tell me you have beer and not the fucking craft shit like you ordered at dinner the other night."

"I'll have you know that craft beer is amazing, and I'm just trying to expand your palate with it," he says, coming over to the couch and handing me a good ole American-made beer. While he, on the other hand, has some craft shit he's opening.

"I feel like I don't even know you right now, man. First, the apartment has candles everywhere, your shelves have pictures all over them, and now, you're sitting beside me, drinking something from a place called Wicked Weed."

"Tinley wanted us to have a space that was for us both. Adding a woman's touch isn't so bad. Maybe if you took the plunge, you could see it's worth the fall."

I take a sip of my beer as Ryan continues to rant about how great being a relationship guy is, and it has my head spinning a little. I mean, it wasn't eight months ago that he was sitting on this couch, moping around because the media had taken his relationship with Tinley and spun it to make her out to be some home wrecker for a crazy-ass bitch, Serena. After watching what they went through, it's probably why I'm so paranoid about going all-in with Grace. Her last name alone brings the media, and then lump in my little bit of fame associated with NASCAR, and we could crash and burn quickly.

"Damn, Matt, did you hear a word I just said?" Ryan asks, looking as if I've sprouted an extra arm. "Wow, you really are living in your own world right now, aren't you?" Laughing at me, he grabs the game controller and turns the system on.

As we start to play, my head spins back to Grace. Did I really want more than the two months that we signed up for? Can I be the man she wants or even that she needs?

"Ryan, how did you know that Tinley was it? What made her so special that you thought, 'damn, I can't lose this woman'?"

I look over to Ryan and watch as I know he's thinking back to the relationship he and Tinley had at the start. The smile on his face is growing.

"I guess the moment I ran into her after she went to the drivers' meeting with Grace in Bristol," he declares, smiling at the memory.

"But you literally just met her that morning. How the hell could you have known that she would be worth it?"

"Man, the moment I kissed her between the haulers, I knew she was it for me. My whole body caught fire, and I knew that I would do whatever I needed to protect her and keep anyone away who might hurt her. Did I screw up during our early days? Yep, and the media was rough, of course. But when it came down to it, she was there. When I needed her to be, she was right beside me," he recounts, going to grab a picture.

It's their first kiss. The media caught them kissing and then ran with it wondering who the mystery woman was. When word got out, Ryan thought he'd lost her, but that was just the start of their love story.

Smiling at the image he puts the picture back where it goes and comes to sit back down with me.

"Now, ask me the question you really want to ask," he pushes.

I pull the cold beer to my lips and take a long pull, trying to wrap my head around what I'm feeling and if it's even real.

"I think I might be falling for my fake wife, and it's scaring the absolute shit out of me, man. Problem is, I think she might be falling for me too, but we're both so freaking terrified of admitting it to each other that we're using sex to mask things and having to have this talk.

"Don't get me wrong, the sex is the best I've ever had, and I'm not complaining at all, but I guess we should have a grown-up talk at some point, right?"

Just as I am finishing my statement, I hear soft footsteps coming toward us and know that our guy time is ending. But Tinley could help me. She's Grace's best friend. Surely, she has some tricks to help me woo my fake wife.

"Hi, guys. Nice afternoon off?" she asks, going over to Ryan and kissing him on the cheek.

"Not too bad. Matt was just asking me how I knew that I wanted to keep you forever," Ryan remarks with a smirk that makes Tinley blush just enough that if I hadn't been looking, I would have missed it.

Sitting down between the two of us, Tinley looks at me before resting her palm on Ryan's knee.

"Are you thinking of Grace as more than just a pain in your ass, McCall?" she asks, looking at me like she might chop my balls off if I give her the wrong answer.

I shift in my seat and face Tinley after grabbing another beer from the table and taking a sip.

"Honestly, the more I'm around her, the more I like her. I don't know if that means forever or if that is just right now. We haven't talked about it."

"Well, she'll be with you for the long stretch coming up, so you have plenty of time to find out," Tinley says, like it's so easy and uncomplicated.

"Yeah, so there lies the problem. Sure, she'll be with me in California this weekend, but when we head to Texas, she's flying to Boston to talk with her dad about everything that's going on. And then she and Mila are going to a fundraiser her cousin, Cort, is having for the Boston Revs baseball team."

Tinley looked at me like she had no idea Grace was going home for the weekend. Well, get in line, lady, because that's a fight I've already had.

"Okay, well then you need to tell her how you feel before she leaves for Boston. That leaves us, what, about a week and half to get you on the same page and show her that you're worth the fall too?" Tinley states so matter-of-factly it makes me smile.

Okay, let's do it.

Chapter 19
Grace

Walking into the house after a long day at the shop, all I want to do is kick off these damn high heels and take a bubble bath. I set my purse down and walk toward the back bedroom, where the bathtub is screaming my name. I'm struck by millions of roses covering the living room. What the hell is happening? Did I stumble into the wrong house? Looking around, I can see Matt's trophies and my throw blankets on the couch, so I know that I'm in the correct location. The only question is, why is a florist taking up residence in the living room?

Just as I make my way deeper into the room, I see Matt come around the corner with a glass of wine for me and a bottle of beer for him.

"Hey, Red." He greets me, kissing my forehead. He makes me swoon every damn time, he and that forehead kiss. It's like he has some magic power when he does that.

"Matt, what's going on? Why is the living room covered in flowers?"

"Just wanted to do a little something special for you. I know that you've been working your ass off, getting things for Mila, and that you are meeting with your dad next week, so I just wanted to make tonight about you."

"This is all too much, Cowboy; you didn't have to." Suddenly, I feel shy about all the trouble he's gone to for this.

It may be the most romantic thing I have ever seen, and this man isn't even my real husband. Yet he made the effort and that's what means the most.

Wrapping my hands around his neck, I look up at this gorgeous man who, until today, I didn't realize had a romantic bone in his body, but he just showed up and proved me wrong.

"Cowboy, how about you take a bath with me?" I say just as I turn and walk toward his bathroom.

Just as I get the water running and place my lavender oils in, his arms wrap around me, and I sink into his touch.

Slowly pulling my clothes off, I turn to see him staring at me with a look that I'm not sure I want to label. We've been having such a great time the last few days, and I don't want to scare him off by saying, *hey, umm Matt, I think I'm falling for you even though I said that I would never do that.*

Pulling his shirt over his head, I start to unbutton his jeans, pulling them down his powerful legs, and then removing his boxers. He looks into my eyes, and for just a moment, I think he might say whatever is rolling around behind those eyes. But he bends to turn the water off.

Before I have a chance to warn him that the water is about as hot as a volcano, he sits down in the tub, wincing as he goes.

"Damn, woman, are you trying to burn all the flesh from my skin?" he asks, trying to get comfortable.

"I'll have you know that sitting in a hot bathroom is good for your pores and helps keep your skin looking young," I say before removing my bra and panties and joining him in the molten lava bath.

Sitting down, I lean back into his muscular chest and instantly relax for the first time today. Being with Matt, I find myself being more of myself. More than just the girl who people fear because she doesn't give a shit what other people think and will tell you when you're being an asshole. He makes me feel a little softer, and I think it's because he doesn't take life too seriously.

"This is nice, Cowboy; we may need to make this a nightly thing."

"Ha, Red, I'm not sure my skin can take this every night. I'd lose a layer each time. But if it makes that smile cross your face, I will gladly endure it for you," he murmurs, turning my head and kissing me slowly.

"So, tell me about your day. Was it a productive one?" he asks.

"Well, it was productive and frustrating all in the same phone call. Just when I thought I had found Mila another sponsor, they decided to withdraw just because she isn't a big enough name. And when I tried to sell all her amazing attributes, they wanted nothing to do with her. By the end of the call, I was so frustrated with the man-child, I wanted to curse his family because they're the way any old men's club would be.

"I get NASCAR is a good ole boys club, but at some point, women are gonna come in, and dammit, we need to be given the same opportunities as any man."

Watching her talk so passionately about something and the love that she's given to her position as Mila's head **PR** person, I just feel so proud of her. I wrap my arms around her a little tighter and turn her face to me, kissing the worry of the day away.

Grace is one tough lady, and there's a fierceness she shows just from talking. I know a fight's coming with this sponsor, and

I'm not so sure they're ready for it. But I'm damn sure going to enjoy watching her put them in their place.

My girl is a warrior. Just the thought of saying that phrase out loud makes my breathing pick up some, and I'm hoping that I can keep it in check so she won't pick up on me having a small freak out. But isn't that just what Ryan and Tinley told me to do tonight? Have the talk and see if she's on the same page as me. Can we make a real go of this? Or in less than two months from now, will she be walking away from me?

"Babe," I say, getting her attention as she rests against my chest, sipping her wine. She is the most gorgeous woman I have ever seen, and when she removes the makeup, she is even better. This is the Grace who I always wanted, the one who doesn't want to punch me in the balls at each turn, the one who smiles when she sees me not scowl.

"We need to have a talk before you go to Boston next week. I just want us to be on the same page when you go to war with your dad about this whole deal, okay?" I share, running my hand up and down her arms.

"Okay, I get that, Cowboy," she replies, pulling her legs up to her chest and turning a little to face me.

"We just need to be on the same page about how we ended up in this situation."

She looks at me like I've just thrown the black flag for us to come to a stop.

I move to position her on my lap, and she wraps her arms around my neck.

"Matt, let me be very clear, just in case that Southern head of yours doesn't get it, okay? If you need me to, I'll talk slowly, okay?" She sasses me because she knows I can't resist her when she does.

Smacking her ass, it sends a squeal from her. I can't help but want to punish her when that sassy mouth comes out. It has a direct line to my dick, and the more she sits on my lap in this tub, the more she's going to get just that.

"I am going to tell my dad the truth. The reporter was looking for information, and I stepped in to protect what's MINE. So is that okay with you, big man?" she asks, batting her eyelashes at me.

"So I'm yours then?" I'm desperate to hear her say the words that she told me she'd never say the night we put ourselves in this predicament.

"I'd say after this past weekend in Miami, my mind may have been swayed, and seeing you in another light has me shifting just a little. But that doesn't mean that you don't piss me off on the daily or get on my last nerve with your terrible music choices. You're growing on me like a fungus," she says.

I can't help but laugh at the way she describes me. "Well, I'll have you know that some fungus is tasty, and if I'm not mistaken, you enjoy it." I pull her close again and kiss the hell out of her.

"Well then, I'll have you know, Red, that you are one thorn that I'd willingly keep in my ass if you'll let me because I'm enjoying having you as mine."

"Take me to bed, Cowboy. I'm ready for a rough ride."

I jump out of that tub so fast water runs everywhere. But I couldn't care less. I'll clean that up in the morning.

Chapter 20
Grace

Last week was a bitch. I went out to California with Matt for his weekend race, and now, I'm playing the game of Tetris, getting a whole week's worth of work into three days.

Thursday is D-day, as I like to call it. I fly to Boston to meet with my father, fully prepared to tell him just what's going on and not planning on taking any of his pushback when it comes to Matt. My heart is slowly belonging to my fake husband, and he needs to understand that Matt isn't the man the press make him out to be. The bright side to the weekend is that I do have the fundraiser with Cortney on Saturday, which is going to be the highlight of the weekend.

I'm looking forward to spending some time with Mila since we've only been able to see one another on FaceTime lately. She's been packing and getting ready to move into her townhouse, close to Matt, that we set up for her.

As I finish up the day, I'm still missing a few things when it comes to getting sponsors interested in coming on board with Mila. I make myself a list of the things to do in the morning when I come in. It seems like lately the list is getting longer. Or is it just my worry or my perfection kicking in and me wanting this to go off without an issue?

I drive back toward the house. I knew that today would be quiet. Matt is still out west for the long stretch. I didn't realize that I'd become accustomed to our routines each night. But now that he isn't waiting for me, I take my time driving home.

Walking to the dark townhouse, I find it quiet. That's one thing that I've gotten so used to when I walk through the door. Matt is always playing music. Yeah, I give him hell about his country music selection, but it is growing on me. I've started to add his songs slowly to my own playlist. Guess it's my way of keeping him with me even when I'm apart from him.

I yell out, *"Alexa, play Matt's country playlist."*

The music starts to fill the room, and I notice that the song is one of Matt's favorites. It's an old George Strait song, "Amarillo by Morning." The only reason I know the name of the damn thing is because it came on one morning when I was making our coffee, and Matt decided we needed an impromptu dance session in the kitchen to it. At the time, I thought he was just being silly and wanting to see how I'd react to being so close to him. But the longer the song went on, the more I relaxed into his arms. I enjoyed it, and that may have been the turning point when I started to see him as more than just a fuckboy. He's a good guy. He's just hiding under a man-child.

As the song finishes, I make my way to the bedroom to change out of my work clothes and get into bed. I'm dead tired and don't even have the energy to get takeout delivered. I just want to sleep.

I plug my phone into the charging port and hear it chime as I get comfy to go to sleep. With the time difference in Texas, we've been playing phone tag. But for once, he catches me right before I drift off to sleep.

Hitting the button, I see his gorgeous smile come across the screen.

"Hey, Red. Are you in bed already?" he asks, concern written on his face.

"Hey, Cowboy. Yes, just laid down. It's been a long day. Doing everything that needed to be done in three days is kicking my ass. So how's my driver doing? Staying away from all those pit lizards, right?"

"Yes, Mom. In fact, I'm on my way out to dinner with none other than Ryan and Clint."

"Augh, safety in numbers, Mr. McCall. Keep them in line."

Looking at me, he gives me the biggest laugh. "You do know who I just said I'm going to dinner with, right? Clint doesn't stay in line on a good day. We're going to a public bar. If he doesn't make a scene, then I'll drop to my knees as soon as I'm home."

I pause to think of any comment to say back to that—I have nothing.

"Well, y'all have a great time and be safe, okay?"

"We will. I'll text you in the morning. Sleep good, Red. Night," he says as he ends the call, and I drift off into sleep.

D-day—T-minus twelve hours.

Do not freak out, Grace. It's just your dad. The man who has loved and cared for you your whole life. He's also the man who taught you to be a bulldog and not roll over anymore. Because those are the people who cut your knees out from under you and walk away.

I step onto the plane at Charlotte, my palms getting clammy. Dear God, am I going to pass out? I have flown a million times, and this flight will be no different.

"Miss, can I get you something to drink?" the flight attendant asks as soon as we get the all-clear signs from the pilot.

"Yes, please. A vodka cranberry would be amazing right now."

After taking my glass and drinking the whole drink before she has time to help the passengers behind me, I ask for one more since she's still within talking distance of me.

Walking off the plane, I'm lost in thought when a man I don't recognize comes up to me.

"Excuse me, miss, are you Grace Miller by any chance?" he asks, making me a little uncomfortable that people would know my name.

"Umm, I am."

"I am so sorry; I'm Michael. I work for your father. He sent me to pick you up and take you to your parents' house."

"Okay, Michael. I'm gonna need you to show me some ID, and I'll also need to call my father to make sure before I get into the car with you." I've watched enough Liam Neeson movies to know that I could be sold on the black market at any turn, getting into a stranger's car.

Turning, I grab my bags and hear Michael talking with someone. I can't make out who it is because it isn't on speaker, but soon, he catches up to me, handing the phone over so I can talk with someone.

"Hello, sweetheart. Michael is to take you to the house. I was planning on picking you up but got stuck at work, and your mother is cooking away, preparing for you coming home today," comes my dad's husky voice.

"Okay, Dad, I just wanted to make sure. Can't have your only daughter being sold on the black market. What would that do to the Miller name?" I hand the phone back to Michael before following him to the waiting SUV.

I have always loved Boston; we have lived here my whole life. Most of my family live in New York, but my parents settled just outside the area so that they could drive to New York if they needed to. And I know my parents want me to come home so badly, but North Carolina is my new home, and I'm starting to love that it has adopted me and given me my new family.

Matt may have come into my life in a weird way, and it's all my fault, but thinking back, I wouldn't change what I did. It's starting to turn into one of the best mistakes I've made.

We make our way to my parents' house outside of Boston, and I'm compelled to watch the city roll past me. I have so many fond memories of spending summers with my cousins since they had a house near my parents, and it was always so great. We've always been a close family, and my moving away hasn't changed that. Now, with this bomb that I've dropped on my parents via the press, I'm in survival mode. I think that may be one of the reasons I want to come this weekend while Matt's in Texas. I honestly don't want my family to become attached to him and then a month from now, he's gone, and I'm left to answer a million questions.

Following the tree-lined drive to my parents' house, and I say a silent prayer that tonight will go smoothly. My father is a responsive man, and once I tell him the truth, I'm sure he'll see my reason for having the press think I'm married to Matt. Even though I know I'll get the mother of all lectures about how reckless it was of me to do that. I went to North Carolina to get away from the Miller name and become my own person, yet, in one picture, I've blown that up too.

Pulling up to the beautiful old Tudor-style home, my father comes out the front door just as I step out of the SUV. I thank Michael for the ride and for not selling me on the black market. This causes him to laugh just as I close the door and head to my father.

"Hi, Dad." I greet him before walking up to him as he wraps me in one of his big bear hugs. I relax into his hug and just pause. I love the smell of my dad. He reminds me of old spices and soap. A very dad smell. Ha ha.

"How is my little bug doing?" he asks, looking at me with more concern than anger. And I settle just a little, knowing he's getting on board with what's happening.

"It's been one hell of a few weeks if you want an honest

answer. But starting my new position at Mac has been amazing. The people are so nice, and I'm learning a lot."

"Well, come on. Your mother's been waiting on you all week, and I know she'll want to hear all about it. I better not hog you all to myself," he says with that signature smirk that only I get.

Walking into the house, it's just as warm and welcoming. For most of my childhood, my house was the one my friends wanted to be at. It was because my cousins were always around or maybe because of the amazing lake view we had that I loved spending time out on the water each summer.

I head toward the kitchen and find my mom, pulling a lasagna out of the oven just as I make my way to a bar stool.

"My little peanut is home." My mom comes, rounding the corner to give me the biggest hug.

"Mom, I only moved to North Carolina—it's not like I went off to war, you know."

"Yeah, but you move to North Carolina, then instead of coming to work for our family team, you stay there. Then hell's bells, I find out from the news, not my own daughter, that you married a racecar driver. Darlin', you forget I follow the tabloids like they are my second bible and I've seen things about the 'husband,' and I use that word very loosely. I don't want to see you all over the page because he's strayed," she states, placing her hands on her hips.

Well, that explains where I got that move from. I may have got my dad's aggressiveness in the business world, but the sass is all my mom. Here, I thought it was going to be my dad I would have to defend myself with. Nope, it's the woman standing in front of me.

Rubbing my temples, I can feel the start of a headache coming on, so I close my eyes and count to five. Because if I open my mouth right now, I will say something that my mom is not going to like, nor will it be ladylike.

Taking a long breath, I open my eyes and look up at my mother.

"Mom, I get that you didn't want to find out your only child is married from a newspaper. And to be honest, I didn't want you to know that way either. Yet I also didn't want a random dark-haired reporter trying to drug one of my drivers just to get information as to what's going on at our race shop. So, if you really want to know, no, Matt and I are not legally married. Honestly, we aren't even dating, But am I falling for him? Yep, I sure as hell am, and it scares the hell out of me." I look over at Mom, who's just standing with her mouth open like a fish as I continue.

"Miles was the man I thought I would be with for the rest of my life, and I ended that, so being with Matt now and developing all the feelings I have bubbling over, I'm not sure what to do. If I'm being honest with myself.

"We are trying to keep the media away now. But because of the way he's been in the past and my name, they've taken such a freaking interest that we can't shy away from it now." I unload all the words that I have been keeping to myself for the last month.

"I have the next month to figure out my feelings because at the end of the race season, that's it. We said two months to make sure that his image is what it should be, and I'll help Mila launch her career."

"Sweetie, we know it's been stressful this last month. I know you wouldn't have married someone out of the blue. You may try to play the hard nut at times, but your heart is so big," Mom continues. "True, your dad handled it terribly when we got the news. You have always been so level-headed; we just didn't understand. It came unexpectedly, and then when you avoided our call, and even Jamie's, we were even more confused," Mom says, coming to stand in front of me again. She pulls me into a hug this time, and it's the comforting mom hug that you always want when you know that things have gone south.

Pulling back from our embrace, I look into my mom's eyes.

They're the same as mine, and even though her blonde hair is starting to go gray, she's embracing the change, and I can see what I might look like at her age. And I hope that when I am, I'm half the woman she is.

"Bug, you will never disappoint us. We just want to be a part of your world, even if it's a few states away is all. And I'm sorry for the rough call. I know I didn't give you much room to talk that day and explain yourself. Looking back now, I shouldn't have told you not to embarrass the Miller name. Hell, your cousin, Cortney, has done that enough for the whole lot of you," Dad says, laughing as he joins our embrace.

"Now, let's all sit down, and you can tell us about Matt McCall because the way you just spoke it seems like he may be more than just a right-now," Mom says as I follow her to the small kitchen table sitting off to the side of the living room.

"I know you have your views of Matt, but honestly, I had those same ones until I got to know him. He may be one of the most tender-hearted men I've been around. He cares for his family deeply, and he's worked his way up through the ranks in NASCAR and made a name for himself that wasn't just given to him. The first night I came home to his place after the media article came out, he made dinner for me, and knowing that I have a gluten issue, he made me things that wouldn't bother me. It may have been the sweetest thing I've ever seen. At one time, he stopped what he was doing just to dance with me in the kitchen because I'd had a rough day."

I watched as my parents listened to me talking about Matt, and my mom swooned at certain parts when I told them what he had done.

Looking over at me and placing her hand on top of mine, I saw my mother with tears in her eyes. "My darling daughter, you just spoke of this man as if he's been in your life longer than a month. Those feelings that you are questioning inside yourself—you shouldn't because they are real. You love this man. It may have only been a month, but the heart knows what it wants or needs, and if you listen very carefully, it will bring you to just the place you are to be," Mom states.

I look over to my dad, waiting for him to say something like, *your mother is crazy and doesn't have a clue,* but all he can do is nod along and lean over and kiss my mother's cheek.

"Listen to Mom, bug. There was a time when your mother wouldn't give this old dog the time of day. But I was persistent and finally, she gave in. I got that one date, and the rest is history. Sometimes the best things are when you find what you didn't even know you needed."

My head is spinning. Am I really falling in love? Could Matt be the one I've been looking for this whole time, and I had no idea? Had I loved Miles, or had we just been in the college-lust bubble? Getting up from the dinner table, I excuse myself and head toward my old bedroom. I need a little time by myself to figure out what the hell happened. I went from feeling like I was going to throw up all over the plane on the way here to now having the wind knocked out of me by how supportive my parents were about Matt. They saw the papers and knew that he had a playboy past. But they also knew my judgment, and if I was willing to give him a chance and knew that he could change, then they could too.

Lying across my bed, I dial the one person who will understand my spiral better than anyone.

FaceTime connects faster than I'm expecting, so when her face comes onto the screen, I'm pacing the floor.

"Hey, bestie. How's Boston? It's hot as hell here in Texas. I really wish you'd come. I still don't know a lot of the wives and girlfriends around here, so I'm spending most of my time reading in the hauler, which don't get me wrong, I love. Grace, can you stop pacing around the room? I'm starting to get a little seasick watching you," Tinley says.

"Sorry, yes. I'm just having a little freak out now and need to talk through it with someone who's been in the same spot."

Just as I start to tell her what's going on, Ryan comes onto the screen too. Great, just what I need. He and Matt are very close, and I'm worried he'll run back to him the second I hang up from Tinley.

"Well, if it isn't the married woman. What can we do for you? You do know you called Tinley and not Matt, right?" Ryan says, laughing as he watches me pace the floor of my childhood bedroom.

"Thank you, captain. Obviously, I'm very aware of where Matt is. I don't want to talk to him until I've had my freakout, and I thought that well, hell, since you and Tinley have faced the mountain, why not seek guidance from others? You're his best friend, so you can give me some insight into what he might be thinking since you're here now, I guess."

"All right, lay it on me, Grace. What can we help you with?" Ryan asks.

"Grace, stop pacing and look at us," Tinley calls.

Stopping my movement, I grab my phone. I take a deep breath and prepare myself to unload what I'm feeling.

"Grace, you're kind of freaking *me* out. What's going on?" Tinley asks, looking at me with so much concern. She's been with me since our freshman year of college, and she can honestly say she's never seen me like this.

"I think I may be falling for my fake husband," I mutter a little lower than necessary, but I'm having a hard time getting these words out.

"What was that, Grace?" I hear Ryan ask.

"I said, I think I'm falling for my fake husband." They both pause. Great! I just dropped this bomb and now they have no idea what to do with it. Awesome, that's just freaking awesome. I have lost my mind—completely. Have fallen for the one person whom I shouldn't. Honestly, he may be the one person who could break my heart into a million pieces, and I'll never recover from it. I think that's what scares me the most.

"OKAY, let me make sure I heard what I thought you said, OKAY? You're falling for Matt? Is that a bad thing? You guys are so cute together," Tinley says.

I sit down on the bed and can't help but feel utterly defeated. Matt was just supposed to be a two-month run. Yet here I sit one month into this "relationship," and I have fallen.

"Grace, look at me," I hear my best friend say.

Looking up at her, I see that Ryan has left the frame of the phone, and it's just me and her.

"Sweetie, are you falling for Matt? Hell, I fell for Ryan hard and fast. I wasn't expecting it to happen, but when you find that person who makes you complete, it just happens. Is it just one of the scariest things I've done in hell? Yes. But it's also one of the best because I've found my best friend and partner in him. Have we had our problems along the way? Yeah, but what relationship doesn't? This life isn't for the faint of heart with these men, and I've found that out. I also found myself in the process. So trust your gut and your heart. I know that you thought Miles was the end game, but he was just the layover before you got to your destination," Tinley says.

"Tin, I just don't know if I'm ready to jump in with both feet. Matt is a lot to take, and my family comes with expectations that I don't know if I want him to have to meet."

"Grace, Matt is a great guy. He was just a playboy. Oh, yes, but I've seen the way that man looks at you when you don't even notice. It's something. You should just let go a little bit and take the leap. You may just find what you need."

Tinley is right; I can't live my life scared of ruining the Miller name. Both my parents have seen that I'm falling, and now I just need to tell Matt. Guess when I get back from my trip, it's time to lay it all on the line.

Standing up from my bed, I grab my phone off the bed and hold it up once more so that I can see Tinley. Ryan has come back into the frame and is grinning like an idiot.

"Have fun at the fundraiser with Mila. She can meet some of those Boston Revs. Lordy, I've seen that roaster and talk about drool worthy," Tinley jokes just as Ryan grabs her, throwing her over his shoulder.

Her phone abandoned on the couch.

"Well, okay. Bye, guys. Thanks for the help." I hear Tinley squeal as I hang up the call.

Saturday night and I'm standing in a large ballroom, sipping fancy champagne and hoping I can just hide in the background until it's time to go home. The only reason I've come tonight is to make promotion contacts and introduce Mila to a few potential sponsors.

"This may be one of the biggest events I've been to, Grace. Thanks for letting me tag along," Mila says, coming to stand beside me. The woman is gorgeous on a normal day, but tonight, she's next level. She's wearing a floor-length, dark-purple dress with a slit up one side, and her dark hair is styled into loose curls down her back. As we walked into the event, I noticed more than a few glances our way.

Just as we refill our glasses, my cousin, Cort, finally makes his way over to us with a beautiful red-headed woman.

"Grace, Mila, this is Dylan, my other half and the woman who has finally stolen my heart," he says, and damn, those heart eyes he makes when looking at her are so sweet.

"Dylan, it's so nice to finally meet you. My cousins are talking about you all the time. The woman who tamed The Man Bun here," I say, laughing as my cousin hates that nickname, but it stuck long ago.

"It's just in the stars, I guess. Well, that and the little rug rats we have running around at home."

"Thank you again for inviting us, Cortney. I'm just excited to get dressed up and not be around motor oil for a weekend," Mila says, taking a sip of her drink.

Just as we finish up small talk with Cort and Dylan, I note a very sexy man looking our way. He looks like an Abercrombie and Fitch model in a baseball player's body. Dirty-blond hair is styled exactly right with the slightest bit of highlights. He's clean-shaven and is on the hunt. Lucky for me, he looks like his sights are set on Mila.

"Hello, ladies. I don't think I've seen you around here before. I'm Kyle Bosco. I play for the Revs." He introduces himself with a cool deep voice that I can only assume makes all the women drop to their knees. But he's out of luck with this woman. The only man I'm going to drop for has a Southern accent and makes me scream all night long.

"Hi, Kyle. I'm Mila and this is Grace. You might know Grace's cousin, Cort," Mila says, turning to face him as I walk toward our table to get seated for dinner so she can flirt.

I know about Kyle's reputation. I may not be in Boston but that doesn't mean I don't follow baseball. The man is a known manwhore. But hey, if Mila wants to take a turn on him, she can be my guest. I don't think she should be ashamed for going after what she wants.

Sitting down in my seat, I reach for my phone to check if I have any messages and to get an update on the race.

Matt McCall 10th place—110 laps to go.

Matt's doing great. He was so worried about Texas, but I told him he would do great. He's on an uphill swing and has run great the last few weeks with a win and top-ten finishes. He only has one race left before the cutoff with the final four, and he's sitting in a great place right now.

"Grace, you didn't tell me that literally all the hottest guys on the planet would be in one room," Mila shares, coming to sit with me minus Kyle.

"Ha ha, would that have been a deciding factor in you coming with me tonight?"

I can't help laughing even harder at the face she's making when she sees that Kyle is hunting her down like a dog with a bone.

"Girl, be careful with that one. He can be a handful from what I've heard," I tell her just as he comes to sit with us, remembering I was saying this same thing to myself a few months ago.

The fundraiser ran into the night, raising money for the local women's shelter, and when all was said and done, they raised more than one hundred thousand dollars. It's amazing to see so many people step up and help the community. It's even better to see my cousin finally finding his place now that his baseball career is over. He tells the story that Becket can't run it without him and that's why. But I think it's more that he wants to keep this baseball program running a certain way, and with him at the helm, he can.

I lost Mila about halfway through the fundraiser, and as I'm a good friend, I had text her before calling my Uber to head back to my parents' house.

Me:

Just wanting to make sure you're not in a ditch somewhere and that you're safe.

After waiting to hear back from Mila and wondering if she's off somewhere right now having sex with Kyle, I finally see the thinking bubble pop up on my screen.

Mila:

Hey, girl. Oh yeah, I am just fine. I'll see you back in Charlotte next week.

Me:

You better call me tomorrow. I expect all the details. Because I've heard some things about Kyle Bosco and want to know if they're true.

She sends me a winking emoji and promises to call in the morning.

I order my Uber and wander just inside the building so that I don't need to stand on the street corner where anyone can snatch me. Damn, I've watched *Taken* way too many times; it's making me either paranoid or hyper-aware.

Checking my phone for the final rundown of today's race, I see that Matt has come in fifth today with Ryan finishing third. Clint has ended up tenth.

Just as I get the alert that my Uber has arrived, my phone rings.

Seeing Matt's face come on the screen sends instant butterflies to my stomach. It has only been two days since I saw him, but I have missed talking with him each day and having our back-and-forth banter that has become my routine.

"Hey, Cowboy. I saw you had a top-five finish today. That's great."

"Hey, Red. Damn, you look sexy. Why are you standing outside?"

Blushing at his statement, I reply, "I was waiting on my Uber to pull up when you called, and I didn't want to be rude, getting in while talking on the phone. Hang on, let me get in the car."

After making sure the driver is who he's supposed to be, I slide into the back seat and pick my phone back up.

"You don't look half-bad yourself, Cowboy. Where are you anyway?" Looking at him, I can't see around his body. He's still wearing his racing suit and looks sexy as hell in it.

Giving me that smirk that he knows I love, he slowly starts to remove his racing suit.

"Like what you see here, Red? Missed you at the race today," he says, removing his fire suit under his driver's uniform.

"Tell me again why it is that I needed to be here and you needed to be there. Because that's just too far away. I want to be able to touch you, kiss you, and pull that hair of yours just the way you like when you come," he rasps. My breathing picks up as I pray the driver can't hear our conversation because we're going in a whole other direction than what I wanted, but I am so turned on that I couldn't stop this race car if I wanted to.

As he removes the remainder of his suit, I notice he's in his hauler. Thank God he isn't in some hotel room.

"You haven't answered my question, Red. Now why aren't you with me again?" he drawls in that Southern accent that drives me crazy.

"Honestly, I have no idea right now," I reply with a laugh. My brain isn't firing on all cylinders, and the more I stare at his gorgeous body, the worse it gets. I'm not even able to form a sentence.

"Do you want to know what I think? You ran. You started feeling things and didn't know what to do, and instead of confronting them, you decided to go to Boston. I know you haven't been to a single fundraiser since you left for school. Yet you make an appearance as soon as you can. Does that sound about right, Red?"

"You could be on to something there, Cowboy. But also, I

needed to talk with a few contacts for Mila, and what better way than to kill two birds with one stone?"

"Yeah, so where is Mila? I'd love to say hey. You know, since we are gonna be teammates next year," he questions.

And now I gaze out the window as we make our way down the long driveway that leads to my parents'.

"Funny thing about that—she met someone at the fundraiser and decided to have a little fun before she moves to North Carolina next week," I reveal, paying the driver and then stepping out of the car into the cool air and heading toward the front door.

"Ahh to be single. We'll let her have her fun," he says as I open the front door, coming face-to-face with my mother.

"Grace, darlin', I didn't expect you to be home this early. I heard your car pull up when I was making some tea. Couldn't sleep and thought this sleepy-time tea would help. Ooooh, who are you talking with? Matt? Well then, give me that phone so that I can say hello."

Pulling the phone from my grip, she turns the phone to face her.

"Well, hello there, Mr. McCall," she says, looking over the phone and giving me a wide-eyed look. I know exactly what she's thinking; it is written all over her face.

"Hello, Mrs. Miller. Hope you're having a good night. I was just checking in with Grace to make sure she has a nice night and that she doesn't get into any trouble," he says in his sweet Southern voice, coming over the phone, making my mother swoon just a little at each word.

"You will have to come to Boston soon with Grace so we can all have dinner and get to know you better." Mom continued her ramble for what felt like half an hour. But truly, it was a few minutes because I heard the teapot whistle. Pulling her from her conversation with Matt, I say goodbye and promise to chat more later. She hands the phone back to me.

Looking back at the phone, I saw Matt's smug face and wanted to both punch and kiss him. He was so easy to like, and that Southern hospitality made it even harder to not want to be around him, even more when he made everyone around him at ease. Damn him. Why can't he just be an asshole and not make me want to stay?

Chapter 21
Grace

That wasn't quite the welcome home I had in mind, but damn, the man was so sexy, and when he danced with me in the living room, I was overcome with so many emotions, I just wanted to get out of my head for a moment.

Unpacking my bag and getting things organized for the work week, I make my way outside to sit with Matt as the sun goes down. I know that I need to have "the talk" with him. I need to tell him all these feelings I'm having, but it scares the ever-loving piss out of me to think that he might reject me. Ryan and Tinley made me feel a little better about my thoughts when I talked to them yet again, and Ryan even made a point to say that Matt had acted like a lost puppy during the race weekend. He hadn't even smiled when Tinley had told him the phrase I'd said.

"Hey, babe, got you a glass of wine. Thought we might watch the sun go down," Matt says as I go to sit beside him.

"Matt, we need to have a talk," I start, after taking a long sip of my wine. Maybe if I drink enough, I'll have the courage to talk about my feelings. Knowing that I need to put my big girl panties on, I take a deep breath and lay it all out on the line.

"When we started this, whatever it was,"—I wave my hand between us—"I thought it would be two months of us throwing objects at each other or hurling insults. I never thought it would turn into something."

Looking down at my wine, I can feel myself wanting to shut

down, but I push on. "Matt, you make me feel things that scare the living hell out of me. I haven't been single for long, and I wasn't looking for something, yet I think I may have started falling for you that first night in your hauler. I think I've tried to talk myself out of it. Yet when that reporter tried to drug you to get you in bed, I just knew that I had to do something. Yeah, I got a sentence for being fake married for two months, but I didn't realize it was also going to make me see that my feelings are more than just hatred for the racing playboy."

"Grace," Matt says, pulling my face toward him.

"With you, it's never been a fake thing. I told you long ago that all you had to tell me was that you wanted it all and you could have it. I may have made you think I didn't care one way or the other, but the truth is, I've been waiting for you to catch up. I knew you would get here in your own time. I just had to wait. You make me feel things that I didn't even think I wanted, let alone needed. I was fine with living the single life and winning races. But this last week has shown me that I need something more, and I want the blonde bombshell beside me when all that comes true.

"Whatcha say, Red? Wanna be my *real* girlfriend?" he asks with that beautiful smile he saves just for me.

"Why, you wanna be my boyfriend?" I ask, wondering what line he's going to throw at me.

"So I can kiss you anytime I want," he says, moving in to kiss me lightly.

Letting out a laugh, I reply, "Been watching *Sweet Home Alabama*, have you?" Once again, I'm laughing as he kisses me.

"What can I say? I love me some sassy blondes with smart mouths."

Chapter 22
Grace

How the hell did we get here? If you told me two months ago I'd be Matt's fake wife but real-life girlfriend, I would have told you to go step on a Lego. But now, looking over at the man sitting beside me, I can't think of a better place to be.

"Red, what's going on in that beautiful head of yours?" Matt asks, coming to stand beside me as he finishes getting things packed for us to head out. We decided to make a road trip down to Alabama instead of flying out with the team. Matt wants me to meet his parents and sisters before the race weekend, and to say I'm nervous as hell is an understatement. For God's sake, their son is bringing home a Yankee, so my mission is to impress Momma McCall with all the effort that I can.

"Honestly, Cowboy, I'm scared to death. What if your mom hates me? Hell, I'm not a great cook, and I'm not a Southern lady. She may have thought you'd end up with a Southern belle, and I'm a sassy-mouthed woman who would rather watch action movies than some sappy Hallmark movie," I say, finishing packing up my makeup bag and placing it by the others that Matt has set out for us.

"Grace, look at me," he says in his deep voice that makes me do anything, and I do mean anything, the man wants.

"I don't give a flying flip if you're not Southern or a lady. Honestly, I think that's what pulled me in in the first place. I've had so many women come to me that when you made it a challenge, I wanted you even more," he says, pulling me close to his rock-hard body and kissing me slowly.

I know that if I don't break this kiss, I'm going to have to remake the bed, and that will put us way behind in our drive. Showing what little restraint I have left, I pull away, instantly missing his heat, and turn on my heels, heading toward the front door.

"Very funny, Red. You kiss me like that and then walk away. You do know that I'll punish you for that later, right?" Matt says in that gruff Southern voice that always makes my blood heat up in all the right places.

"Come on, Cowboy. If you're good, maybe you'll get a little treat as we go down the road." I wink at him as I grab my bag and close the door behind me just as I hear him mumble a "fuck me," pulling the remainder of the luggage behind him.

Four hours later, we're only an hour outside the tiny county where Talladega Speedway is located. Why the hell we thought this was a good idea, I'll never understand. My back hurts from being in the car for so long, and I had to pee about an hour ago but didn't want to mention that to Matt as he made a point to tell me to make a pit stop before leaving, but I ignored him in favor of thinking I could make it longer than I actually did. So now, here I sit, miserable because of my own pride. But we used the time to dive a little deeper into each other's history. Since we had done this relationship a little ass backward, we figure it's only fitting to find out more.

"Look out that window, Red. That's one of the biggest speed-ways we go to each year. Are you ready to stand beside me this weekend? As a real couple?"

"Cowboy, if the last two months have told you anything, it's that I'll follow you into that whirlwind and smile as I do it."

We keep driving for another forty minutes to Matt's home-town. He may not have grown up with the same life I did, but from just listening to him talk about his parents and sisters, I can tell they are close. He's made something of himself, and yet he wants to make sure that his family is taken care of more than anything else.

"All right, Red, this is it. Are you ready for some good ole-fashioned Southern hospitality?" he asks, showing me that million-dollar smile again. He is so excited to see his parents and siblings that it's infectious and helps calm my nerves just a little bit.

Coming around to my door, he helps me out of the car, and we walk hand in hand up to the front door of a beautiful, white farmhouse with a big, red wooden door and a big, Southern wrapped-around porch. I can see why Matt purchased this house for his parents. He saw that his mom would love sitting out on this porch either reading or just rocking in the big, white rockers.

Just as we get to the front door, it bursts open, and out run two smaller kids and a tall, blonde woman who I can only assume is Matt's sister.

She slows as we approach, closing the door behind them. Her eyes grow big as she takes in the sight of her brother. Did he not tell them we were coming?

"Matty, is that you?" the blonde asks as Matt releases my hand and goes to give her a hug.

"Hey, sis. Where the hell are you running off to so quickly? I think I just got a glimpse of my niece and nephew as they blew past me—not even stopping to say hey."

"Yeah, sorry about that. They were raised in a barn, you know. No manners whatsoever unless they're with Mom, and then it's like they're the Queen of England's kids."

"Tracy, this is my girlfriend, Grace," he says, turning to me as I stand behind him, watching the kids run toward what I guess was his sister's car.

"Girlfriend, huh? The media says y'all are married. She's not your wife, Matty?"

I like this woman. She doesn't give a shit who he is, or even me for that matter.

"Yeah, well, the media likes to spin things all the time. Why don't you come have a drink and we can fill you in on all that's gone on in the last two months?"

"I'd love to, but I've got to get the kids to soccer practice. But I'll see you at the race on Sunday. I wouldn't miss the hometown boy taking on the big bad super speedway." Giving Matt a kiss on the cheek and me a hug, she leaves to find her kids.

We make our way into the house, and as soon as I step foot in the door, I instantly relax just a tiny bit. It smells just like when I went home to Boston two weeks ago. That's one thing about having a mom who cooks. All the kids want to be a part of that house, and you can tell that Matt's mom is no different.

"Come on. We better make our way into the kitchen before she comes to find us and I get in trouble for lingering outside the room."

Music is playing softly over the speakers, and just as we turn a corner, I notice a sight that makes me tear up.

Matt's parents are in the middle of the kitchen, dancing. Now things start to make sense of why the man is so damn charming. He watched his parents growing up, and it's clear why the man always listens to old country music and why he always pulls me into dancing with him as we cook together. He's been watching his parents all this time. And I am just in awe of this man. He is romantic and doesn't even have to try. He just learned what to do from the man spinning this petite woman around.

Clearing my throat, I can't help but feel my heart swell at the sight of my parents. I've watched them dance in the kitchen with one another for as long as I can remember, and to see them now still doing the same as they always have done makes me glad that Grace has wanted to dance with me in the kitchen as well.

"All my stars, is that my son? My married son who I had no idea was even dating, let alone married." Mom starts to rant when she notices Grace standing beside me.

"Matthew Thomas McCall! Why the hell didn't you tell me you were coming and bringing my beautiful daughter-in-law with you no less?" she says, smacking me on the arm before bringing me into one of her amazing hugs.

"Sorry, Mom. Believe me, Grace wanted to tell you we were coming, but I wanted it to be a surprise," I reply with those big puppy dog eyes that she can't ever stay mad at.

Pulling away from me, she turns to Grace.

"Well, Miss Miller, or should I say Mrs. McCall? It's nice to finally get to see my daughter-in-law in person instead of in a magazine or a texted photo from my son," my mom says.

"It's really great to finally meet you too, Mrs. McCall," Grace says.

"So what are you and Dad doing besides dancing in the kitchen?"

"We were getting ready to head out on the boat. Did you folks bring your swimsuits?" Dad asks as he grabs an armful of beers from the fridge to put into a cooler.

Looking at Grace, she shrugs as if to say, *whatever you want, I'm game.*

"Sure, let me just grab our bags, and we can get changed. Meet you down at the dock in twenty minutes."

"All right, kids. We'll see you down there. And, Matt, no sex under my roof, got it? I shouldn't even have to say that, but I know how my son can be when he has a beautiful woman in front of him. Hell, I was young once too, kids," I hear my dad say as we make our way to the guest bedroom. I'm sure Grace is five shades of a tomato from my dad's comment.

Chapter 23
Matt

After changing into our swimsuits, we headed out toward the dock. I had always loved being home. My parents had bought a boat long ago, and I had learned to wake surf on it. That was partly the reason why I had my own.

After helping Dad unhook the boat, we head out onto the lake. I made my way over to sit with Grace, who was in deep conversation with my mom. She instantly stops talking the moment I drape my arm over her shoulder.

"And what are you two talking about? I bet it was about me, seeing as you stopped as soon as I sat down."

"I'll have you know, we were talking about Grace's job and everything that's about to change with Mila joining the ranks next season," Mom said.

As the boat comes to an alcove, my dad slows it, and Grace gets up to move, but I pull her back to me. I can't resist kissing her and making sure she's doing okay with meeting my family. I get that it could be overwhelming. Hell, I'd only met Clint and Jamie and they had me stressed out.

Once I release her hand, she makes her way to the front of the boat where my dad is getting the fishing gear out.

"Matty, you seem happy, darling," my mom says, turning her gaze to me. I know she can see the stupid look on my face from just seeing Grace.

"Never in my life did I think this day would come. Grace is

changing you, isn't she? She's making you become the man I knew you had inside you. The man who you have never wanted to be."

"Yeah, I think she is, Mom. What started out as something neither of us wanted has turned into something that I'm not sure I can live without now. She makes me want to push myself both on and off the track."

When I look back at my mom, I see her wipe her eyes.

"Just be careful, Matty. Love can be a minefield. If you step right, it's beautiful, but if you step wrong, it will blow you five ways to Sunday. But I can see by looking at that girl that she's all in."

I walk toward the front of the boat and meet Grace's gaze as my father continues to talk with her about how to cast a rod and when to reel it back in.

We spent the rest of the day on the lake, fishing, catching up, and just enjoying time with my parents. They made it so easy to relax, and by the end of the day, Grace had become one of the family.

As we say our goodbyes, my mom promises to see us at the race on Sunday, and Grace makes sure she has her cell phone number so they can get together during the race.

"I thought we were staying at your parents' house, Cowboy."

"Nope, this was just a pit stop before we get to the real destination."

During the drive back toward the racetrack, I had booked us a room for the night. I know that she doesn't mind staying in the trailer with me, but I want to show her that I'm the man she wants to be with.

I put the key into the lock of the room I booked for tonight but let her go first because I want to see her reaction.

"Oh, wow, Matt. This is beautiful. When did you have time to even do this?" she murmurs, walking into the room as I follow behind her.

"I have my ways, Red. Sometimes, it's nice just to be surprised."

"Look at you being romantic. I'm glad that gene didn't skip you. That would have been such a shame. A hot sexy man who isn't a romantic would have been terrible," she says, pulling me close to her.

"Red, you make me want to be a lot of things that I didn't want any part of. People can change for the right person. Just remember that, babe."

Crushing her mouth to mine, I kiss her how I've wanted to all day. The five-hour car ride was pure torture. I lift her into my arms, and her legs wrap around me so naturally, like we've always been doing this.

I walk us over to the table, laying her out. I can't wait another minute; I need to be inside this woman now. Pulling her leggings down, I notice she doesn't have any underwear on.

A small growl comes from my throat. "Red, have you been bare for me all day, when I couldn't touch you?" I groan, making my way down her perfect body. I can smell how turned on she is, and it only makes me harder the slower I move down her.

Finally, I reach her clit, sucking a little harder than normal, and she nearly jumps off the table. "Seems that someone needs an orgasm. Huh, Red. Tell me. Do you want me to fuck you, or would you like for me to eat this pretty pussy until you're screaming my name?"

I'm a greedy man, and knowing her, she would say she wants me to fuck her, but my siren isn't going to be getting what she wants yet. I'm going to torture her just to the edge and then fuck her so deep that she milks my cock dry.

I get to kissing the inside of her thighs, close enough to her clit that when I blow small breaths onto her, she shivers from the contact. I moan, and the next time I repeat the motion, I move my tongue over her entrance. I've waited long enough, and I need to taste her. As I lap up all her sweetness, her hands come up to grip my hair. I knew she was getting close when she started to grind her pussy on my face, making me pick up the pace just enough to get her even closer. I insert one finger and pump in and out. Her cries get louder.

"That's it, Red, scream for me. Show everyone who you belong to," I growl, inserting another finger into her as I suck her clit into my mouth.

I feel her start to climax, and I pull out, ripping my boxers down and slamming into her in one motion. I bury myself in her so deep that my balls tighten. Damn, she is so hot. I'm going to come if I don't start moving. So I pull her toward the end of the table and pump into her—hard. She arches her back off the table, and I pull one of those perfect nipples into my mouth just as I feel her start to orgasm. Grabbing her around the neck, I make her look at me, right as she comes. I thrust into her two more times, and my release comes barreling into me, and my legs nearly give out.

When I look down at Grace, I see she has that post-sex glow and my cum is dripping out of her. It makes me smile so big. I scoop her up and head toward the bathroom, wanting to stay in our little bubble that we created tonight. Because the media was back in our faces at the racetrack this weekend. I knew they would be asking questions and wanting to know more about us. We avoided them for a little while after the news broke. But with the final two races of the season coming up, the media needs something to talk about, and because both Ryan and I have made the final four, the media wants to know more about the playboy and the PR girl.

After taking a bath and wrapping Grace in a fluffy towel, we head to bed. Today went better than I could have expected. My parents love her, and I can finally start to see my future outside of racing, and this blonde bombshell is starting to be a big part of it.

I pull the towel from around her, drawing back the covers in the king-size bed, and I motion for Grace to get in.

"You're not putting any clothes on tonight, Red; I want you naked just in case I wake up in the middle of the night so I can have you any way I want you," I say as I smack her on the ass and lay her down. She rolls onto her side and makes room for me beside her.

Snuggling her into my side, I turn on the TV to find a movie for us to watch as we drift off to sleep.

Chapter 24
Grace

Yesterday was overwhelming to say the least. Matt's family was amazing and reminded me a lot of my own. His mother has a heart of gold, and when she hugs you, you just melt into her and feel safe, exactly like I do when my own mother hugs me. Our moms will be close when they finally have a chance to meet one another.

I know I need to dress the part of the race car driver's girlfriend as I pick out my outfit for the day. The media is going to be following us, not only because they think we are news, which is still silly to me because honestly, we're boring, but also because Matt is a part of the final four with his teammate, Ryan. Which is so exciting, especially because Tinley will get to hang out with me while they attend the press and signing event.

"Ready to go, Red? We need to head out in about ten minutes," I hear Matt say as he comes into the room to make sure we have all our bags ready.

"Keep your pants on, McCall. I'm trying to find an outfit that says NASCAR wife but also doesn't scream, 'Girl, what the hell were you thinking?'"

"Babe, you look good in everything. Just throw on some shorts and a 'Matt McCall' shirt and call it a day. It's hot as Satan outside; you're not going to want to put a lot of effort into your outfit. I promise, you and Tinley are going to want to stay in the AC all day until we have to make the pit walk."

I pick my favorite vintage McCall shirt that I stole from Matt's closet my first few nights at the house and pair it with some cute shorts and my Vans. When I make my way out to the living area, I find Matt on the phone with a deep frown forming on his face.

"Cowboy, what's wrong?" I ask as I go to stand next to him.

"It's nothing, Red. My guys were just calling to let me know that there was an issue with the inspection, and unless they can get the spec right, I'm going to be starting at the back of the pack, which is the last thing I want to do at this track. It's easy to get caught up in the big one, and being a part of the final four group, honestly, a wreck is the last thing I want to think about with this race. It's never good to tempt fate," he says, wrapping his arms around me.

I can feel how tense he is, and I want to take that away from him, but there is nothing I can do. The cars go through a machine full of sensors to make sure that everyone has the same components in place. We just need to have faith that the team will make the necessary changes so the car can go through the machine again and pass. Time will tell if that's going to happen.

Chapter 25
Matt

My day has gone from one I was looking forward to to one that I just want to get over with as fast as possible. I thought everything was taken care of back at the shop when I left on Wednesday to come to visit my parents. And I thought that the car would sail through the inspection with no issues, but I guess dreaming is child's play.

"Cowboy, look at me," I hear Grace call out as I put our luggage into the trunk of the car.

I round the back as I close the trunk. Running her hand through my hair, I instantly start to relax just a little.

"Listen to me carefully, driver, okay?" Her voice is sexy—the one that she uses when she wants to be dominated.

"You are going to be great out there, and this is just a little bump in the road." She gives me a little peck before trying to walk away from me. Grabbing her wrist as she turns, I pull her back to me again and kiss her with so much intensity and with all the emotion that I want to share with her but don't because I think it will scare the ever-living hell out of her.

"All right, Red, get in the damn car before I fuck you where the whole world can see." I smack that beautiful ass before she makes her way to the passenger seat, and we head toward the track.

It's going to be a good day, no matter what. I have the sassiest-mouthed woman beside me who wants me to do well, and honestly, I think I may just be falling in love with her.

Walking into the garage area hand in hand with Grace, this time around feels different. The atmosphere is electric, and everywhere I turn I feel like we're being watched because we are. If it's not for the fans wanting to get close to the cars, then it's the media snapping pictures of Grace and me.

"Grace, Grace, can we get a quote before the race?" I hear one of the reporters say as I walk over to check my car.

She looks up at me. "I'll be right back. Let me appease them so they'll leave us alone, Cowboy," she says, giving me a quick kiss as she walks toward the vultures.

"Hello, gentlemen. You have, looking down at my watch, five minutes, so fire away," she says to the reporters as I go over to find out what the hell went wrong in the inspection.

It turns out that the mistake isn't as bad as I thought when they called me earlier to let me know that we were at risk of heading to the back of the pack. Turns out I was missing a lug nut. It may have come off when they were unloading the car. But that just goes to show that even the smallest detail could cost me the race and the possibility of the championship for Mac Motorsports.

Looking over at Grace, I can tell she's deep in conversation with one reporter, and it looks to be getting a little heated, so being the good boyfriend/husband I am, I make my way over to her. She isn't a damsel in distress, and I know she can handle herself when needed, but the raise of her voice as I get closer doesn't sit right with me.

"Jim, what's going on here, to make my wife talk over you?

"She was happy to answer your questions, but I'll gladly walk away and leave you standing here," I demand, instantly feeling protective of what's mine and making sure that this asshole knows that I mean every word.

"Well, if it isn't the playboy himself. Mr. McCall, care to answer my question that your wife refuses to?" I'm immediately on edge and in defense mode. Being on the edge with car issues, the last thing I need is some reporter with an ego.

"And what exactly is that, Jim?" I cross my hands over my chest, ready for this asshole to crawl back to the pit he came from.

"I was just asking Grace here if she was part of a long line of women who became a notch on your belt or did she think this was real. Because from where I stand, you're not really married." The asshole has the nerve to smirk as he continues to talk.

Letting my hands drop to my side, I feel my fist ball up, and I want to throttle this asshole faster than a two-hundred-mile-an-hour car, but I need to keep my cool. My contract is worth more than me beating the total shit out of this reporter.

I walk right up to him and make sure he's looking directly at me. There are times in your life when you realize what you want, and this is one of them.

"Listen closely, Jim. I'm not going to repeat myself, so get that recorder ready," I say, deadly serious.

"Grace belongs to me, mind, body, and soul. She's not, nor has she ever been, a notch on my belt, as you put it. She's my first love and my last. So if you ever question my devotion to *my wife*, I'll make sure those credentials around your neck never appear again. Do I make myself clear, Jim?" I say, backing up just a little to grab his lanyard and inspect which media outlet he's with.

With wide eyes I see him start to speak.

"Thank you for your time, Mr. McCall. And Mrs. McCall, I'm extremely sorry for making you feel less than and overstepping," he says as he turns on his heels and heads off to bother someone else.

"Cowboy, I had that under control; you didn't have to swoop in and be my knight in shining armor."

"Babe, I know you were fixing to serve his balls up on a plate, but some battles you don't have to do alone." Wrapping my hands around her waist, I bring her close.

"Plus, it was hot watching you get a little flustered," I say, kissing her forehead. "Now, are you ready to go to the trailer for just a little while so I can rest and then get ready for the race?"

The walk back to the hauler is quiet. We were only stopped a handful of times by fans wanting an autograph or picture, and those I'm always happy to do. The fans are what makes our sport what it is. It may have started off with moonshiners but the ones who brought it into the light were the ones who sit in those stands and cheer the ones going over two hundred each weekend.

The hauler is like a second home to me, and I enjoy the space. While sitting down on the couch, I hear a knock come from the door. When I get up to see who it is, I'm surprised to see Ryan and Tinley at our door. The man is all about routine on race day, and to see him out of his box is different. As I look down at my watch, I can't resist giving him shit that he isn't checking off his to-do list.

"Ryan, aren't you supposed to be rubbing a cat or something right about now?" I say with a smirk.

"Don't you worry, I've already taken care of that pussy," he says just as Tinley smacks him in the stomach as she walks by him toward Grace, who's taken the seat I was just in.

After catching up with Ryan and Tinley and filling them in on the encounter with the nosy reporter, it was time for us to get ready for the race.

With Grace by my side, I walk toward my car, feeling at peace. She makes my worries wash away. Rubbing her wrist with my thumb as we listen to the national anthem, I know that I only have one thing left to do before getting in my car and going to work.

"Give 'em hell, Cowboy," Grace says before wrapping her hands around my neck, waiting for my kiss.

"I love you, Grace Miller," I say, taking her breath away and seeing tears well in her eyes.

"You sure, Cowboy? I know I'm a pain in the ass and have the mouth of a sailor sometimes," she replies, her smile growing as she speaks.

"I've never been more sure of anything in my life. You make me want to be a better man, and with you by my side, I'm gonna make every dream come true that you've ever dreamed because you deserve it."

"Matt McCall, damn you," she says, tears spilling from her beautiful eyes.

"I love you; I think I have since the moment I took a chance on you in that hauler. You are just made from a different stock, that's for sure. And that may be the reason why I've fallen so hard that it scares the hell out of me."

Kissing her one more time, I pull back once again because it's time to go to work.

"I just wanted you to know that before I go to work," I say, climbing into my car.

She blows me one final kiss, and I watch as Grace makes her way over to Tinley and they head toward the pit area.

As I walk up to Tinley, I'm smiling so widely.

"Girl, you look like you ate a clothes hanger," Tinley says.

"Thanks for that, Tin. Honestly, I'm just happy is all."

"And why would that be, lady?" I know she wants me to spill all the details, and I will tell her in time, but right now, I want this moment to be just between Matt and me. The media have taken so many firsts from us that this one we'll tell in our own time.

Talladega Speedway is one I both love and hate. She is a big mother of a track, and you put in thirty win-hungry men and it's a recipe for disaster. The big one is bound to happen with cars bumping into each other before passing or slow cars not knowing when to get the hell out of the way.

After one hundred laps, we only have fifty to go. I've had a decent run today, but I lost a good many positions on a late pit stop.

The team tried to get me back where I needed to be, but I've had an uphill battle all day.

"Crash in turn three. Looks like it's the big one. Go low, Matt. You gotta stay out of it," I hear my spotter say just as I round the corner, dropping low and barely missing a car as it spins past me.

"Yellow flag is out. We have ten laps left and a shit ton of cars to try to get around if you wanna have a chance of winning," my crew chief says over the headset.

After riding around for five laps, as they cleaned up what

looks more like a junkyard than a racetrack, the flag attendant was giving us the green flag coming signal when we came around under our final caution lap.

I pull my straps just a little tighter and brace for the next four laps. I'm sitting in tenth. It's doable at this track to slingshot that many cars, but I'll need the extra help. Ryan is a few cars back, so if we can line up, maybe it could work.

As we round the third turn, my spotter makes me aware that Ryan is on board to help if he can get to us in time. Now it's go time. We'll get the green-white-checkered flag this time around.

Gassing it as I pass the flag stand, I swing to the outside and head toward the lead car. I can feel the air grip as I get close to the next car, but I don't take my foot off the pedal. I'm a man on a mission, and finishing as close to first as I can is my number-one job.

Just as we get the white flag, I see Ryan in my rearview mirror and know it is go time.

As we make our way out of turn two, Ryan taps my back bumper, giving me just enough push to send me diving under the lead car.

Crossing in front of the car, I see the finish line so close I can taste it. I push the car to its limit and cross the line just ahead of the pack.

I did it! The local boy from small town Alabama had taken down the beast.

Just as I slow, a voice comes over the headset.

"Cowboy, I'm so proud of you. I knew you could do it! Now come to Victory Lane so I can kiss you. Oh, and Cowboy…I LOVE YOU!" Grace says as the headset disconnects.

Making my lap around the track, I slowly head toward Victory Lane, and putting my car into park, I climb out of my car to celebrate.

I won the race but what I really won was the girl of my dreams. She is worth all the media and all the news articles. She makes me want to be the man she deserves, and I will spend the rest of my days doing just that.

Epilogue
Matt

3 Months Later

I'm standing at the back of the press room, watching Grace turn on the charm for the media. She called the press conference to officially welcome Mila into the Mac Motorsports family. Never in my life would I have ever guessed that Grace would have taken a chance on me, let alone agree to marry me for real this time. The last few months have been a whirlwind with the season ending. I didn't win the championship this season, but hell, I think in the end, I may have ended up with something even better. Then we announced to our families that we're getting married in Hawaii during the off-season.

After finishing fourth this year, I'm ready for a break and time to enjoy my gorgeous soon-to-be wife on a beach for the next week, and I'm itching to get out of here and just be us.

"Thank you to everyone for coming. We at Mac Motorsports look forward to the season ahead and what Mila will add to our team," Grace says just as the cheers erupt from those inside the press room.

It's a big deal to bring a female onto your team, and honestly, one I'm happy to be a part of. My contract has been extended for another five years, and I'm ready for the next chapter in my life.

"Hey, Red," I say. Walking up to my gorgeous girl, I pull the hat off my head that I put on earlier to hide that I was in the room. I wanted this day to be about Mila and Grace, not about me. Yeah, I know that's shocking since I seem to lap up the attention from the media.

I turn around and am hit by the beautiful smile that blew me away all those months ago. Hell, I think I may have fallen for her when she threw those books at my head. That may have sealed my fate, and I fell in love with her even more when she gave me the chance.

"Ready to become Mrs. McCall, Red?" I say before kissing her. I hear clicks go off and know that I hadn't waited long enough for the press to leave, but hell, I'm a man, and my woman is within reaching distance, so I'm going to kiss her, pictures be damned. Throwing caution to the wind, I pull her even closer and dip her, just so they'll have a new picture. We started this relationship in the press, so why not give them one more shot before I officially make her my wife for real this time?

Heading for the door, we say goodbye to Mila, knowing we'll see her in a few days. She's become one of Grace's closest friends, and she's a part of our wedding party. After getting to know her as a teammate, it's easy to see why everyone loves her. She has a passion for racing and makes me and Ryan push each other even more. And she balances out our team so well.

We walk toward my Dodge Charger, and I grab Grace again because I can't get enough of this woman. "Red, you ready to spend forever being a pain in my ass?"

"Oh, Cowboy, I'm just getting started," she says before giving my already hard cock a rub, then strutting toward the passenger side door and getting in.

Damn, this woman. What may have started off as a joke and was to be nothing has turned into the best mistake of my life. And I'm going to make sure she knows how much I love her for the rest of hers. The media may have thought it was for show, but

Grace was my checkered flag long before she even gave me the green one.

One night was all it took for me to see what I didn't even know I wanted. This NASCAR playboy is off the market, ladies and gentlemen, and I'm never looking back. And I'm damn happy about it.

It's funny how life can change in the blink of an eye. Or in my case, the snap of a picture.

THE END

DRIVING with *Heart*

HALEY COOK

The final book in the Driving Series
is coming this November.

Ride along with Mila and see just how fast her story can be.

Pre-Order Now
Driving with Heart

Acknowledgments

An with that, book two is done. When I started writing Ryan and Tinley, I never imagined that Matt and Grace would be in my head next. But here we are, and I am so excited for everyone to read their love story.

To my husband Ereck, thank you for helping with the NASCAR bits. I know you thought I was crazy when I asked questions about the track or what the pit crew side of things were, but hey, it helped.

To Jenni Bara, thank you for letting me use the Miller family name and characters—they were so fun to be a part of. And thank you for helping when I needed you to look over this one and find the places where I needed to add more.

To Annie Charme, thank you for reading over my words and helping with scenes that needed just a little extra.

To my beta readers, Kelly, Kayla, Shani, and Ashley, thank you so much for reading over my story and letting me know where I needed more sassy Grace or steamier Matt. I have loved the process with you ladies in my corner.

To Cadwallader Photography—Katie, thank you so much for the beautiful image and for helping pick the one that worked perfectly. So here's to the next one coming soon.

To Storm Wilson, thank you for being the face of Matt McCall. And being a part of this process, for being so sweet when I bugged you, letting you know I was going to be tagging you—a lot.

To Samantha from Sammie Bee Designs, thanks for bringing my cover to life yet again. I love it more each time I see it. Who would have ever imagined being a reader, one day, I would ask you to bring my cover design to life? I couldn't have asked for a better partner in this adventure, and both covers are beyond anything I could have asked for.

To Kat's Literary Services (Kat & Louise y'all are amazing), thank you so much for putting up with me and editing my story. You make me a better writer. I'm so glad you took a chance on my writing. I know you might have gotten tired of me saying, *umm…I'm gonna have to move the date yet again*, but you never made me feel bad for doing it, and that means a lot to me.

To the readers…thank you for taking the time to read my story. Being a reader first, I know you have so many options for what to read; if you chose mine, I am forever grateful. I know the story may not be perfect, but for this baby author, I'm so glad you wanted to read it.

Becoming a writer wasn't something on my radar, but I've just started writing. Book two has been a work of love, and I'm so glad that the words finally came together and you have them in your hands now. Enjoy! Haley

About the Author

Hi, everyone. I'm Haley (some of you may know me as The Southern Librarian in the book community). Married to my best friend, I'm the mother of two teen boys. I grew up in small-town North Carolina and still live there now.

Racing has been in my blood my whole life; my dad taught me how to count using race cars and then took me to tracks when I was a little girl. I met my husband at a local dirt track. So it's easy to see that I would write a NASCAR trope.

Stay tuned for what's to come, and I hope you enjoy this ride with me. I never thought being a writer was something I would be able to achieve or share my stories, but one day, I started writing, and these books are the product of that one day.

DRIVING SERIES

Ryan & Tinley's Story

Order Now:

Driving Force

Matt & Grace's Story

Order Now:

Driving Wild

Chase & Mila's Story

Order Now:

Driving with Heart

DRIVING Force

HALEY COOK

Chapter 1
Tinley

"Y'all—I DO NOT WANT TO GO!"

Ignoring my protest, I'm thrust into the shower. "You're going—kicking and screaming if that's what we have to do," Mia declares. Having been my best friend since freshman year at App State, she knows when it's time to get me out of the house. "You need a day out away from books and working at that library surrounded by more books. It's your last year. Enjoy college for a change."

What's wrong with liking books? I think to myself.

"Tin, I know what's rolling around in that little head of yours, and yes, books are fine, but you need other things in your life. Like boys and boys and more boys," she points out.

"Mia, you know I'm the girl who is invisible to boys or the one they friend zone, right? I may be the quiet girl, but I'm not as shy as some may think. I just don't let people get too close because I don't want my heart broken."

"That's where you're wrong, Tin. You just don't let them see you and the awesome person you are because you have read so many romance novels that no man can ever live up to that idea of the perfect partner."

It's easy for her to say. Her dark brown hair, big blue eyes, and curvy figure make the boys stop and take notice anywhere we go.

"Ugh. Okay, fine, I'll go." I give in, but my less-than-pleased tone makes my reluctance very clear.

Living with my best friends for the past three years, I understand that we usually have the most fun when they get me out of my comfort zone. Mia, Grace, Lily, and I might be very close, but you build a complex quickly when you're the single girl and everyone else is coupled up. I can't help if I get lost in my studies more than hanging out with the six of them. My Saturday nights usually consist of the girls getting ready for dates and me reading the latest book on my Kindle instead of being the seventh wheel.

And yes, I know what you're thinking - *Don't they have hot friends to set you up with to go along with them?* The answer is yes, they do, considering they are all dating guys on the baseball team. But their guy friends always seem to see me as the chubby girl who makes them laugh, not girlfriend material. Don't get me wrong, they have all been super sweet, but it's always the same thing. "I like you, but I just think we are off as better friends." So, it never goes further than the first date.

If they are dragging me to God knows what today, I better put some effort into it, or I'll, as my mother says, *die alone with a cat*—by the way, I don't even like cats—then it'll eat my face off. Since I'm alone, no one will find me until it's too late. Insert face palm emoji here, please.

After finally pulling myself out of the shower and drying off, I'm met with three pairs of eyes staring at me like I'd just said I was Team Jacob instead of Team Edward.

"Umm, ladies, what's up?" I no sooner get the last word out before different clothing options are thrust at me like I've never dressed myself before.

"Okay, let's slow down. Of course, I have some questions. First," I lift my hand, "where are we going? And second, why are all three of you so excited about this?"

Lily is the first to chime in. She's usually the quieter of the four of us, the normal southern girl. Auburn red hair, dark green eyes, and the sweetest personality you will ever meet. Even if she told me she planned to kill me in my sleep, she's so sweet I wouldn't believe it until it happened. This explains how she landed James, the star baseball player, two years ago. We are all sure she'll follow him to whichever farm team he lands at after the draft in a few months.

"Ok, so don't kill us, but we're going to a NASCAR race," Lily tells me, a little too excited for my taste.

Pausing to let it sink in a little, I finally reply, "Umm, y'all know I like quiet places, right? I mean, I work in a library and want to go into publishing when I finish school. In what universe did you think this would scream, 'Hey, Tin will love this and will put up no struggle whatsoever about going?'" I ask, looking at them quizzically.

"Yeah, yeah, we know you like boring," Grace chimes in.

Yes, Grace is that friend, that bitchy girl that will always say what she thinks even if no one wants to hear it. She has blonde hair, green eyes, and wears her signature red lipstick, ready to cut any man who might impede her because she gets what she wants.

"But guess what, Tin? You're going! I pulled some strings, and a family friend who does PR for a team is letting me get some experience for my PR/Social Media class. He got us all passes to the Food City 500 Race in Bristol, Tennessee since it's only an hour from here."

Knowing I don't really have a choice, I shrug. "I better get dressed, then. Yee haw, make me a NASCAR pit lizard, I guess. Show me what I've been missing all these years."

None of my friends find my sarcasm or exaggerated Southern accent funny. Instead, they pounce on me like lions in the jungle that just found their last meal. When they finally give me an inch of breathing room, I turn to look at myself. The dark colors of the royal blue fitted tee and dark-washed jeans enhance my curvy figure, but my favorite part is the signature sparkly chucks that I always wear.

"Let the games begin, bitches!"

Grace does her Breakfast Club fist bump in the air. Lily stands back, jumping and clapping, and Mia just shouts, "Hell yeah, you are smoking hot!"

I don't know about smoking hot, but I feel better than average with my hair done in loose curls and a little makeup applied. The humidity living in North Carolina can be rough, so it's best to just go natural.

Going to a race might be the craziest idea known to man because I know I'll be out of my element. But my girls have all the confidence in the world, making me smile and hold my head higher. Just as we walk into the living room, a knock comes from the front door. Lily heads toward it like she has a beacon on James and knows his every move–but I've always been told that it's the quiet ones you've got to watch out for.

James no more gets his foot in the door than I realize I'm once again the seventh wheel. Lily and James are so cute it would make anyone sick. When James settled down, his buddies wanted that same thing, so that's how Mia and Grace fell for his best friends. Here I sit, a single girl in a room full of couples. Then, out of the corner of my eye, I notice a guy I haven't seen before trailing behind Miles. Granted, it's hard to see around Miles. Standing six foot three and built like a linebacker, he takes up a lot of space. James is the shortest of the bunch by a few inches. It's hard not to look at them and see why my best friends are lucky women. Internally kicking myself for being so picky. Great, not only am I going to a sporting event I know nothing about, but now I'm being set up on a blind date. Yep, where is the wormhole I can jump in?

"Okay, are we ready to go? I need to see what the huge deal is with NASCAR."

Miles, Grace's boyfriend, is the first to chime in. "You're going to love it, Tin. Fast cars and beer. What's not to love?"

"Miles, you know me so well." *Just kill me now,* is what I really mean, but I give him a playful smile.

The next thing I know, James is pushing a handsome man with blonde hair and light green eyes in front of me. If I were a betting woman, I'd say this is one of his athlete friends based on his build alone.

"Tinley, this is Chase, and no, he does not play any sports before you even ask. Well, not at school, anyway. I know you're tired of athletes. Even though I should be hurt by that, I'm not. He's in my sports medicine class."

"Hi, Tinley." Chase reaches out to shake my hand. "It's nice to meet you. James has told me a lot about you. Thanks for letting me tag along to the race today."

Lordy, this man is nice to look at. His sea-green eyes could make a girl lose all train of thought and whereabouts when his attention is on them. Maybe it won't be such a bad day after all. "It's nice to meet you, Chase. I would love to say that James and Lily have also told me all about you," I laugh a little, "but they didn't. I'm so sorry."

"Well, if I had known that James had such a beautiful friend, I would have made sure he had given me your contact sooner." I can't help but blush at the statement. Chase may just be what I was looking for, or maybe he could help me figure out this racing shit my friends thought I needed to understand.

As we follow the others out and load up into Miles's suburban, I tell myself to just enjoy today. Even if it kills me. And between NASCAR and a blind date, it just might.

Want more of Ryan & Tinley's story
Grab your copy now.

Available on Amazon & KU

Driving Force

www.ingramcontent.com/pod-product-compliance
Lightning Source LLC
Chambersburg PA
CBHW061521120726
48001CB00004B/1376